Murder at Freedom Hill
An Edmund DeCleryk Mystery

by
Karen Shughart

This book is fiction. All characters, events, and organizations portrayed in this novel are the product of the author's imagination or are used fictitiously. Any resemblance to actual persons—living or dead—is entirely coincidental.

Copyright © 2022 by Karen Shughart

All rights reserved. No parts of this book may be reproduced or transmitted in any form or by any means, electronic or mechanical, including photocopying, recording or by any information storage and retrieval system, without written permission from the author, except for the inclusion of brief quotations in a review.

For information, visit our website at:
www.cozycatpress.com

ISBN: 978-1-952579-52-3

Printed in the United States of America

10 9 8 7 6 5 4 3 2 1

Dedication:

To my husband, Lyle, for his ongoing and ever-present encouragement, support, and love. To my publisher, Patricia Rockwell, for her confidence in me, encouragement, and kindness.

Acknowledgements:

Where to begin. There are so many people to thank for helping to make my dream of writing the Edmund DeCleryk cozy mystery series a reality.

My family: husband, Lyle; children: Jessica Hurwitz, Jeremy Hurwitz and our daughter-in-law, Debbie; siblings, Alan Green and Marcy Brody, and their spouses, Joan, and Jim, for their ongoing support and encouragement.

Members of my community: Wayne County (NY) District Attorney Michael Calarco; our friend, Jim Quinn, retired Rochester City policeman (and husband of my dear friend, Mary, one of my beta readers); the Sodus Bay Historical Society, and the Village of Sodus Point, NY, for providing information about the Underground Railroad and Maxwell Settlement, upon which Macyville is based.

My beta readers: Lyle and Jessica; and dear friends Cheryl Davis, Mary Quinn, Shelley Usiatynski and Deb Vater. John DiLeonardo, who narrates my books for Audible, for his technical advice and terminology to use for the audio descriptions of the exhibit at the Lighthouse Cove Museum. I borrowed the term ROMEOs from Aaron Hurwitz. Read on to learn what the acronym means.

In Memory:
My brother, David Green, who will always have a presence in my heart, and Nova, our sweet rescue beagle who recently followed the real Gretchen over the Rainbow Bridge.

Prologue One
Macyville, a settlement near Lighthouse Cove, NY
   November 1859

A few miles west of Lighthouse Cove, Abraham Butler and his wife, Miranda, stood side-by-side, each holding the hand of a young child, as they watched a procession of men, women and children scurry down a steep, narrow, rocky path surrounded by a thicket of woods, the trees barren of leaves, their branches skeletal and forbidding. The eerie sound of a screech owl pierced the silence.

At the bottom of the path, on the beach, villagers escorted escaping slaves onto rowboats waiting to transport them to a schooner that was anchored a hundred yards out on Lake Ontario. Some, hobbled from age, physical abuse, and many miles of treacherous travel, were aided down the embankment by the younger and stronger of the group.

Like bees flitting about on a lazy summer afternoon, a soft humming permeated the air: spirituals sung of hope and salvation; prayers invoked for protection and peace. The captain of the schooner, 57-year-old Samuel Weatherfield, placed his right index finger over his lips, a cautionary warning.

Weatherfield and his friend, Hiram Ward, ushered the runaways onto the small sailing ship. Babies whimpered; children, sleepy and disoriented, stared wide-eyed, not comprehending what lay ahead; the women pursed their lips and the men, with trembling hands, tried to remain stoic.

It was a cloudy night with gentle winds blowing out of the south and an occasional glimmer of a fingernail moon, a good portend for a successful journey. Eighty miles north across the lake, freedom awaited in Thomastown, United Province of Canada, named in memory of Thomas Battleforth, one of its most prominent citizens.

Abraham's sister, Betsey, had started down the path with the others, then at the last minute turned around and ran back up the hill to hug the brother with whom she had recently been reunited.

"Sister, we'll see each other again." Abraham gave her a gentle shove. "For now, you must get on that ship." Betsey started to cry.

Brother and sister hugged once more; then Betsey ran down the hill to the beach, climbed into the rowboat that awaited her, and shortly after, scrambled onboard the schooner just as the sails were unfurled. Abraham's eyes welled with tears.

Gathering their children closer, he and Miranda watched the ship as it began its slow journey across the lake. If the weather and wind held steady, by dawn it would be in Canadian waters and its passengers would be free.

Lurking in the shadows, in the woods, a man with cold, angry eyes planned his revenge.

Prologue Two
This Century-November

For residents of Lighthouse Cove, NY, November was always a month of mixed emotions.

There was a yearning for the blazing colors of October, the cool, crisp nights, starlit skies, bright days. For a low-hanging sun that could still warm the bones and ease the joints. For the farmstands, now shuttered until spring, that had offered up a bounty of ripe produce, local honey, homemade baked goods and jams, fresh herbs. For the hayrides and bonfires and deer spotting among the apple orchards. For the unbridled joy of chattering, costumed children extending small hands for treats as their parents kept a watchful eye, glowing lights illuminating their way.

There was also the peace that comes with tourists gone for another year and the ease of getting about. The sound of waves, ambling onto the beach like lazy sloths. The geese and swans gliding effortlessly around the bay, no longer competing for space with boats and bathers, and the eagles soaring silently above on currents of wind. The rumbling and grumbling of street noises now muffled by a thick carpet of brown, fallen leaves.

There was excitement and anticipation, too, in November. For a day, later in the month, when families would gather to give thanks and then soon after, start to prepare for the hustle and bustle of the upcoming holiday season. For the hunters who had been looking forward all year to donning their camo, retrieving their guns, and stalking their prey in fields and woods, hoping to bestow upon their loved ones a largess befitting of their labors.

For some, November was also the month of grieving. A month of decay that precedes death. Where what was past was past and would be no more, and what lay ahead was the chill and dark of winter.

Chapter 1

Alex Butler, former school superintendent and current mayor of Lighthouse Cove, NY, looked at the clock on his nightstand. It was 6:30 a.m. and he'd been awake for two hours, listening to the steady patter of rain on the roof.

He stretched, got out of bed, walked over to the window, opened the blinds, and watched as thick coal-smudged rain clouds slowly drifted west giving way to a low narrow band of pale pink, shimmering in the east. Just then his cell phone rang. The caller, his wife, Cheryl, was an intermediate school principal who'd been away at a conference in Albany for the past few days.

"Alex, did I wake you?"

"Hi, Cheryl, I've been awake for a while. Why are you calling so early? Are you okay?"

"No, I'm not. I couldn't sleep after our conversation last night. I'm concerned about you."

"Honey, please don't worry. I'm fine." Alex, a trim man of medium height with tawny skin, curly black hair, and clear green eyes, sighed, regretting that in a weak moment he had confided to his wife that he had something to discuss with her after she returned home. He reassured her that all was well; still, he knew she was anxious.

"Can you please tell me what this is about?"

"It's too complicated to talk about over the phone, Cheryl. Please don't fret. I promise, we'll talk tonight."

"What time will you be home?" she asked.

"By mid-to-late afternoon. Remember, I have that field trip with the college students today."

A member of the Lighthouse Cove Museum and Historical Society board of directors, he'd been working with its executive director, Annie DeCleryk, to restore a settlement where abolitionists and freed people of color had lived from the 1850s through the 1920s and where runaway slaves had boarded ships that sailed them to freedom across Lake Ontario to Canada.

"What time will you be home, Cheryl?"

"I expect by 4:30. I'll be leaving here as soon as I get dressed and have some coffee. I'm meeting with the superintendent at noon and need to get back to prepare for it and have a couple other meetings after that. Please be safe, Alex. I love you."

Alex said he loved her, too, showered, dressed, ate a light breakfast, and watched half-an-hour of the morning news on cable TV. Then, grabbing a light rain jacket that hung on a hook on the coat tree in the foyer, he gathered up the items he would need for the day and started out the door.

The rain had finally departed with the passing dark clouds; the temperature had fallen. At the last minute, he hung the jacket in the back of the closet and pulled out a warmer one. With a touch of regret, he thought, *"I probably won't be needing this until spring."*

Chapter 2

The sun was coming up over the horizon at 7:30, and by now a band of brilliant rose-gold stretched as far as the eye could see.

Ed DeCleryk, former Navy SEAL and retired Lighthouse Cove police chief turned criminal consultant, was spooning freshly ground coffee beans into a French Press when his wife, Annie, ambled into the room, her blue eyes still blurry with sleep.

"Morning. Have you fed Gretchen?" The petite woman ran her right hand through her short, tousled grey hair, yawned, and bent down to pet their beagle, who'd been sleeping on her bed next to the kitchen table.

Ed nodded and bent down to kiss his wife. "Tea?"

"PG Tips, please."

"Milk and honey?"

"Yes, I'll add those myself. You always give me too much honey and not enough milk."

"Honey for my honey," Ed, blue eyes twinkling, responded with a smirk, then proceeded to turn the kettle on.

Annie rolled her eyes.

"A little grumpy this morning, are we?"

"Not really, but I have a busy day. Alex is meeting Eric Klein and some of his students at Freedom Hill this morning at 9:45 to see where the slaves fled to Canada, and after that they'll come to the museum to tour the Macyville exhibit. We'll be doing the same dog-and-pony show later this afternoon, for a group of high school students."

Eric Klein, the son-in-law of Ed and Annie's deceased friend, George Wright, and his wife Sally, was a professor at the University of Rochester whose area of expertise was the abolition movement and the Civil War.

Ed handed his wife a mug of steaming tea. As she poured milk into it and added honey, she said, "Eric originally planned the trip to Freedom Hill for September, but I convinced him to postpone it until the exhibit was completed at the museum and more of the buildings at the settlement were constructed.

"After their tours today of Freedom Hill and the museum, they'll stop at Macyville on their way back to Rochester. Since I can't be with them, I alerted the construction foreman. He asked me to text him when they were on their way and said he'd show them around."

"How's the construction going?"

"We're making progress. Unless there are unexpected delays, we should be in good shape weeks before the grand opening on July 4. Ed, you haven't seen the exhibit yet. If you have time today, why don't you join us?"

"I might just do that. I don't have anything on my schedule other than making a trip to the hardware store for some supplies so I can start restoring the antique wardrobe you bought for the back bedroom. What time should I be there?"

"We're going to show them a short introductory video and give them lunch before they take the tour. If you want to watch the video and have lunch with us, 11:00 should work."

"That's perfect; it'll give me time to go to the hardware store. I can start the project tomorrow."

Annie glanced at the clock on the wall, "I have a couple of things to do before I head over to the museum. As much as I'd prefer to linger and chat with you, my dear, I need to get moving." She stood on tiptoe to kiss her tall, lanky husband. "I'll see you later."

Chapter 3

Ed showered, dressed, and walked Gretchen; then he puttered around the restored ship captain's house that stood on a bluff overlooking Lake Ontario. A few minutes before 10:00 as he was driving to the hardware store, the police scanner on his cell phone squawked. Seconds later, he heard the dispatcher announce that a caller had reported finding a body at Freedom Hill.

Hearing sirens and spotting flashing lights in his rearview mirror, he quickly pulled over to the shoulder of the road as the emergency vehicles and a police car sped past him. Curious, he followed them into the parking lot and watched the EMTs and the medical examiner, Mike Garfield, jump out of their vehicles and start to run down the path to the beach.

Lighthouse Cove Detective Brad Washington stayed behind to talk with Eric Klein and his students, who were clustered together next to a beige University of Rochester van. When Brad noticed Ed get out of his car, he said something to the group, excused himself and walked towards him.

Over six-feet tall, the handsome, brown-skinned detective had clear hazel eyes, dark hair clipped short and sported a trendy five o'clock shadow. He was wearing jeans, a black turtleneck sweater under a hefty military-style brown leather jacket, and polished black loafers.

The two men greeted each other, then Ed said, "I was heading to the hardware store when I heard the dispatcher over my scanner. What happened?"

Brad shook his head. "Tragic situation, Ed. Alex Butler is dead. He was shot."

Shocked, Ed responded, "How awful. It's hunting season, and the wooded area where hunters are permitted is no more than a couple hundred yards from here. Could a stray bullet have hit him?"

"Don't know yet, but the students are traumatized. I asked them to wait inside the van until I'm ready to speak with them."

"Who found him?"

"The professor and his students. They planned on meeting Alex here in the parking lot at 9:45. When they arrived, they saw a car they assumed was his, but he wasn't here. They figured they'd gotten their signals crossed and he was on the beach waiting for them. They discovered his body halfway down the path."

"I know Eric. He's the son-in-law of our friends George and Sally Wright."

"I thought his name sounded familiar. I was studying for my detective exams when you investigated George's murder. I remember you interviewed Eric because you had some questions about the War of 1812, but that wasn't his area of expertise."

"Good memory."

"Did you know about the field trip this morning?"

"Yes, from Annie. I was supposed to join them at the museum after they were done here."

"Ed, I need to meet up with Mike and the EMTs. Walk with me. If the mayor' death wasn't an accident, I expect you'll be asked to assist us with the case, and it'll be good for both of us to hear what he has to say."

The two men caught up with the first responders and watched as the medical examiner kneeled on the ground to examine the body. Alex Butler had fallen backward. His green eyes, now cloudy and lifeless, stared up at the men; his jacket was unzipped, his turtleneck had been pierced by a bullet at the base of his throat, and puddles of blood soaked the knees of his jeans.

Wearing an unbuttoned khaki trench coat over black slacks, a blue cotton shirt and black Doc Martens, the burly ME greeted them somberly then motioned to Brad, who squatted beside him. "Alex was killed by slugs that came from a 12-gauge shotgun."

Brad asked, "How could you determine that so quickly?"

"From years of experience. Entry wounds from a rifle would be much smaller."

"Do you have any idea about the time of death?" Ed asked.

"My best estimate is between 8:00 and 9:00 this morning, rigor mortis hasn't quite yet set in."

"A 12-gauge is used for hunting. Could his death have been accidental?" Brad asked.

"No. If his death was an accident and stray bullets from a hunter's gun killed him, the entry wounds would be random, not targeted, like these are. It appears the murderer was quite skilled; I'm positive he was shot from a distance. If he'd been shot close-range his head would have been blown off. The first slugs hit him in the knees so he couldn't run away; then the killer finished the job by shooting him in the throat. Whoever did this wanted Alex to suffer before he died." The ME shook his head. "What a cruel and heartless thing to do."

Ed said, "He must have planned on meeting someone before the students arrived, with no idea that his life was in danger."

Mike pushed back the shock of brown hair that had fallen over his forehead. "I'm sure you'll figure it out. In the meantime, I need to get his body to the morgue to conduct an autopsy. Once I remove the slugs, I'll call the techs so they can transport them to the forensic crime lab in Williamson."

"Did you find any personal effects?" Brad asked.

"Yes. His wallet and keys."

The detective donned gloves and placed the items in an evidence bag that he'd removed from his jacket pocket. "What about a cell phone? A log of incoming and outgoing phone calls and messages might help with the investigation."

Mike shook his head. "No phone."

"It could be in his car," Ed suggested.

Brad replied, "Ed, let's go interview Eric and his students and then let them get out of here. After that, we can check the mayor's car for his phone."

Eric got out of the van first, greeted the investigators, spoke with them for a few minutes and then motioned for the students to join him. They huddled around their professor, visibly shaken. Brad pulled a small digital voice recorder from his pocket and recorded their contact information and answers to his questions. None of them had noticed anyone else at the scene when they arrived nor had they seen anything suspicious.

The investigators watched the van pull out of the parking lot, then headed toward the mayor's car. It was unlocked, and after searching every nook and cranny for several minutes, they came up empty handed.

"It's hard to imagine that Alex didn't have his phone with him. I bet his killer took it," Brad remarked.

He pulled his phone from his jacket pocket, called the police chief, Carrie Ramos, and as he was talking, smiled and gave Ed a thumbs-up.

"I'll let him know. You'll call the crime lab in Williamson? They'll need to get here as soon as possible. Thanks. Yes, I will."

He walked back to where Ed was waiting.

"Ed, as I expected, Carrie would like you to work with me on the investigation. She wants to know when you can start."

So much for restoring that wardrobe, Ed thought. "I can start right now."

"I need to get back to the station to write my report. Can you stay and secure the scene and wait for the forensic techs? I have a crime scene kit in my car."

"I can. Then I need to go over to the museum. Annie is expecting the mayor and Eric and his students around 11:00 and I want to let her know about Alex's death before she hears about it from another source."

"Carrie will notify Cheryl Butler," Brad said, "and ask about the cell phone. After that, she's going to schedule a press conference for this afternoon and wants us to be present. I'll text you with the time once I have it."

Chapter 4

Ed watched Brad drive away and remembered a recent conversation he'd had with Annie, who revealed that she'd heard through the grapevine that he'd become engaged to Felicia Delgado, the morning news anchor on one of the local TV networks.

With her willowy figure, large, almond-shaped chocolate brown eyes and sleek dark hair cascading to her shoulders, Felicia supposedly was the envy of all the eligible women in Lighthouse Cove, especially Terri, the pretty red-haired server at Bistro Louise, who'd flirted mercilessly with the detective, despite his pointed lack of interest.

One afternoon a few weeks ago, Annie and her friend, Eve Beauvoir, had met at the Bistro for lunch. After taking their orders, Terri had confided how disappointed she was when she'd learned about the engagement. She had never given up hope that someday Brad might succumb to her charms.

Ed's cell phone rang, interrupting his thoughts. Carrie's number appeared on the caller ID.

"Hi, Ed. Brad says you're on board to help find Alex's killer. This is his first murder case since he made detective; it'll be good experience for him to work with you."

"Thanks, Carrie. I expect he'll be a quick study. He mentioned that you're going to schedule a press conference for this afternoon and would like us to be present."

"Yes. The media has probably already learned about Alex's death from listening to the scanners, but I want to get the facts to them quickly to avoid rumors. Brad will confirm the time with you.

"As soon as we're finished with this call, I'm going to head over to the intermediate school to notify Cheryl

Butler, hopefully before any reporters contact her. Then I'll come back here to write the press release. After the press conference is over, let's take the rest of the afternoon off and meet tomorrow morning for a strategy session."

"The forensic team should be here shortly, Carrie. I'll start securing the site and show them where Alex's body was found. Then I need to get to the museum to talk with Annie."

After moving his car across the road, Ed placed yellow crime scene tape along the path at Freedom Hill where the mayor's body was discovered and around the perimeter of the parking lot. He recognized tire tracks from the emergency vehicles, his and Brad's cars and Eric's van. As he looked more closely, he noticed another set of tracks near the entrance. Unfortunately, the driver had parked on the grass and the tracks were muddy from last night's rain. There would be no way for the forensic techs to determine the type of vehicle that had parked there.

Chapter 5

Several minutes later, Carrie arrived at the intermediate school. Sue Eldridge, Cheryl Butler's administrative assistant, was sitting behind a desk outside the principal's office and greeted the police chief.

"Good morning, Chief Ramos. Do you have an appointment with Principal Butler? I don't remember seeing anything on her calendar; she's preparing for a noon meeting with the superintendent."

"I don't, Mrs. Eldridge. Is she available? I need to speak with her."

"She just got back a little while ago from a conference she was attending in Albany. Is something wrong?"

Without responding to the question, Carrie asked, "Could you please tell her I'm here?"

"Oh my, did something happen to one of her children?"

Carrie shook her head. "No, but it's important."

Looking concerned, Sue picked up the phone and announced Carrie's arrival.

Cheryl opened her office door and smiled, her brown eyes crinkling at the corners. Like her husband, she was of medium height and slender. Her honey blonde hair, cut in a straight chin-length bob, was parted on one side, and tucked behind her ears. She wore a sage green cashmere turtleneck over a long black woolen skirt and black, low-heeled boots; her only jewelry a wide gold wedding band, a slim gold watch, and small gold hoop earrings. "Hi, Carrie. Come on in. What can I do for you?"

Just then, Carrie's phone rang. She recognized the caller ID and answered it. "Hi, Mike. I'm at the intermediate school. Can I call you back?"

"This won't take long," the ME responded.

She turned to the principal, "I need to take this call," she said, excusing herself and walking outside the building.

"Now I can talk. What's up?"

Mike explained that he'd conducted a preliminary examination and verified that Alex had died almost immediately after being shot through the throat; that the slug had migrated into one of the chambers in his lungs, and the two others were embedded in his kneecaps.

"Can you send the slugs to the forensic tech office in Williamson?"

"Already on it."

"Thanks. Brad's back at the station writing his report, and Ed's securing the site. He'll be assisting us with the investigation. Please give me a call if you find anything else that will help us find Alex's killer."

Cheryl was standing by her desk, frozen in place, when Carrie entered her office.

"You should probably sit down, Cheryl. I have something to tell you."

Several minutes later, after summoning Sue to her office to inform her that Alex had been murdered, the principal wiped her eyes and composed herself to answer the police chief's questions.

Chapter 6

Cheryl was stumped. She simply couldn't figure out who would have wanted her husband dead. When asked about her whereabouts the evening before, she verified that she'd been at a conference in Albany and had driven back to Lighthouse Cove earlier that morning.

She produced a receipt from the hotel with her check-out time, 7:30. She understood the police chief would need to rule her out as a suspect. She volunteered that she'd spoken with Alex twice—last evening, before he went to his weekly poker game with his friends—and again this morning at around 6:30.

"He's been a little off lately, and a bit preoccupied. He said he had something he wanted to discuss with me tonight but refused to talk about it over the phone."

"Did he sound upset or frightened?"

"Not at all, he sounded…. surprised. I have no clue what he wanted to tell me, but I can't imagine it had anything to do with threats against his life.

"Even though he assured me he was fine and there was nothing to worry about, our conversation this morning was a little tense. I'm so glad I told him I loved him before we hung up." She started crying again.

"Ed DeCleryk is going to assist with the investigation. He'll be working with our detective, Brad Washington. One of them will call you in a day or two and set up an interview."

"Who found my husband's body?"

"The professor and students who were supposed to meet him at Freedom Hill for the field trip."

"What a terrifying experience for those young people," Cheryl responded with empathy.

"Is there anyone I can call for you?" Carrie asked.

"No, thank you. My sister and Alex's live nearby. I'll call them and ask that they stay with me until my kids get home and help me break the news to the rest of the family."

"Where are your children?"

"Jesse and his wife, Sara, live in Batavia where they're second-year English teachers. Leah is a senior at Cornell; after she graduates, she's planning to go to veterinary school. Daniel is a sophomore studying computer science at SUNY Buffalo. They'll be devastated."

"Are any of your parents still alive?"

"Yes, both sets, and they're retired. Mine live in Florida and Alex's live in Arizona.... How in the world do I tell his parents they've outlived their healthy son?"

"I'm so terribly sorry this has happened to you and your family," Carrie said somberly.

Cheryl asked, "When will the medical examiner release my husband's body? He's to be cremated, and we'll need to make those arrangements."

"I'll ask that he notify you as soon as the autopsy is finished. It shouldn't take more than a day or two. One more thing. Alex's cell phone is missing. When you get home, could you check to see if it's there and get back to me?"

"Even if he were in a rush this morning, it's odd he would have forgotten it, Carrie, but yes, I'll check and let you know."

She paused. "Do you know where Alex's car is?"

"It's at the parking lot at Freedom Hill. Once the forensic techs are finished with it, someone will bring it to you.

"Cheryl, would you like me to drive you home and stay with you until your family arrives?"

"That's very kind of you, but I'll be fine. We only live three blocks away; I can drive home by myself."

Sue had been sitting next to the principal, holding her hand. She said, "You shouldn't be alone, Cheryl. I'll follow you home and wait with you. Please, no arguments."

"Thank you."

Carrie expressed her condolences again and then drove to the police station where she began writing the press release and collecting her thoughts for the press conference.

Chapter 7

The forensic techs arrived at Freedom Hill just as Ed had finished securing the site. They would check for fingerprints, collect hair samples and trash, and search for other clues that might help the investigators solve the crime. Once he was sure they had everything they needed, Ed got into his SUV and headed for the museum.

The brilliant sky at sunrise had made way for clouds the color of brushed pewter that hovered over the roiling silver lake. The day looked like an antique photograph: sepia, gunmetal grey, milky white and black, faded like withered grass. The direction of the wind had changed, picking up speed from the northwest, with fallen leaves swirling around the museum parking lot as Ed pulled into a spot. The temperature had plummeted—winter silently creeping in like a cat about to pounce upon its prey.

He entered the building and was greeted by Martha Kelly, one of the museum's docents, who along with her husband, Patrick, ran the gift shop.

"Hi, Ed. Annie said you were joining us this morning; you're early, the rest of the group isn't here yet."

"Is Patrick working today? What about Jason?"

"Patrick has a doctor's appointment and will be in later today. Jason's upstairs in the library." Noticing the grim expression on Ed's face, Martha asked, "Is something wrong?"

"Can you please call Jason and ask him to meet us in the boardroom? I have sad news I want to share with all of you."

Martha looked alarmed. She called Jason, then locked the door to the gift shop and followed Ed down the hall.

On a long table at one end of the boardroom, Annie was arranging trays of wraps and subs, cut vegetables, a basket of chips, cookies, and bottled drinks. Jason arrived, looking concerned.

Smiling when she saw her husband, she said, "Oh, hi, Ed. I was just starting to set up for lunch. You're early."

She paused when she noticed Martha and Jason standing quietly beside a somber-looking Ed.

"Is something wrong?" she asked.

Ed sighed. "Yes, and I wanted to tell the three of you at the same time. Alex Butler was murdered this morning at Freedom Hill; Eric Klein and his students found him. I was just at the site and will be assisting with the investigation."

Martha gasped, Jason looked shocked, and Annie started to cry.

"Any idea who killed him?" she asked a few seconds later after wiping her eyes.

"No. Carrie is scheduling a press conference for this afternoon, hoping it will result in someone coming forward who saw or heard something that could help us. I'll be working with Brad, and she'd like us both to be there."

Martha remarked, "This *is* terrible news. I need to get back to the gift shop and call Patrick." She turned to leave the room; her shoulders hunched.

"I'll come with you, Martha. I think Annie might want a few minutes alone with Ed," Jason said.

Chapter 8

Ed hugged Annie as she wept. "He was such a decent man, Ed. I can't imagine why anyone would want to kill him."

She wiped her eyes, paused for a second and said, "I just thought of something, although I feel horrible mentioning it right now. Did you happen to find a USB drive or laptop in his car?"

"No, nor his cell phone. Why?"

"When we curated the exhibit, Alex recorded an introduction about Macyville and for human interest, information about four of his ancestors who lived or were sheltered there until they escaped to Canada. A couple weeks ago, we realized we'd forgotten to add a conclusion. Alex recorded it last week and was supposed to bring it to me on a USB drive before the exhibit opened to the public over the weekend, but he's been preoccupied lately and never got around to it.

"He apologized and said he'd bring it with him today, and we could install it while Eric and his students were eating lunch. He'd also subscribed to an online ancestry site and had been working with a genealogist to find others, like him, who were direct descendants of his Macyville ancestors so we could invite them to the grand opening.

"That list was on his laptop. We were going to copy those files onto my computer and another USB drive for safekeeping while the students were taking the tour. Now, except for the audio descriptions we already have and portions of the grant he helped to write, it's all gone."

"Annie. It's possible he intentionally left the drive and his laptop at home and planned on getting them before coming here."

"Today's schedule was tight. Ed, he wouldn't have had time to go home after the tour of Freedom Hill," Annie argued.

"Carrie had planned to ask Cheryl about the phone. I'll text her about the laptop and USB drive."

A minute later, he looked up at his wife. "Done."

"Ed, we're naming the visitor's center at Macyville for Alex; it was to be a surprise. Now he'll never know how much we appreciated all he did for us. I feel sick about it." She started crying again.

Her husband changed the subject. "How about if I help you clean up the boardroom? What would you like to do with the food?"

Annie wiped her eyes, opened a drawer in a sideboard and removed some paper plates. "Would you mind putting some of it on these? I'm not the least bit hungry; Martha and Jason might be. If you have time after you leave here, can you take what's left on the trays to the fire and police stations? I assume it won't be wasted and they'll appreciate it."

"I'll do that. Are you going to cancel the tour with the high school students this afternoon?"

"I don't think I can. They're spending the morning in Rochester touring Underground Railroad sites, the grave of Frederick Douglass, and the Susan B. Anthony House. They'll be eating lunch in the city before coming here.

"By now, I expect everyone at the school district is aware of Alex's death, but probably no one thought to call the teacher, and I don't have his cell phone number. When he and his class arrive, I'll pull him aside and tell him about Alex's murder. He can break the news to his students, and they can decide what they want to do. Ed, I need to contact my board members about Alex. Are you sure you're comfortable delivering the food? If you have other things to do, I can send Jason."

"I'm heading in that direction anyway. I want to talk with Carrie about the case before the press conference starts. After that, I'll go home, feed and walk Gretchen and start dinner. Any requests?"

"This morning before I left, I put the ingredients for a beef stew in the slow cooker. It should be done by the time we're ready to eat."

"I'll make a salad."

Annie blew Ed a kiss. "Thanks."

She sighed. "What a horrible day."

Audio #1-Introduction

In the mid-1800s, during the height of the abolition movement, Lighthouse Cove physician Benjamin Macy dedicated 60 acres of fields and woods he owned along Lake Ontario for the establishment of Macyville, a settlement for freed persons of color and those who supported the movement to end slavery.

The main house, where he and his family lived, was visible from the road. The other homes, businesses, a schoolhouse, and a Quaker meeting house, were protected by a ring of trees and later, for added protection, a stockade fence.

The property also served as a stop on the Underground Railroad. At the northern end, a steep hill descended through woods to a broad beach below where escaping slaves boarded a schooner that would transport them across the lake to Canada. They named it Freedom Hill.

As you tour the exhibit, you'll discover lighted glass display cases with memorabilia and artifacts excavated at the construction site; view digitized copies of maps, letters, and photos; and listen to audio descriptions about four of my ancestors who lived at Macyville or passed through on their way to freedom in Canada: Abraham and Miranda Butler; Betsey Cooper, and Hiram Ward. You'll also learn what happened to the settlement after it was abandoned in the 1920s.

An illuminated acrylic sculpture at the end of the tour, created by local artist Donald Chambers, is shaped in the wings of a dove, and etched with the names of all those whose lives intersected at Macyville. We hope you'll enjoy learning about a notable period in the history of Lighthouse Cove.

Chapter 9

Carrie ran across the street to purchase a to-go cup of cappuccino at Bistro Louise for a much-needed burst of energy in anticipation of the press conference, scheduled for 2:30. She was exhausted. She and Matt had been awake for most of the night trying to calm their fussy 18-month-old-son, Arturo, who had an ear infection. He'd finally fallen asleep when their three-year-old, Natasha, awakened at 5:30, full of boundless energy.

She walked back across the street and met Ed and Brad as they were heading down the hall towards her office. Barbara, the receptionist, intercepted them.

"Carrie, Cheryl Butler called. She said she got a text from you asking her to look for Alex's laptop and a USB drive along with his cell phone. She wanted to let you know she couldn't find any of them."

"Thanks, Barb." Carrie turned to the two investigators. "Before we determine the killer took them, I want to search Alex's office at Village Hall.

"Cheryl said he'd been somewhat preoccupied lately. Maybe he stopped there before going to Freedom Hill and on his way out forgot to take them with him."

"Annie said the same thing, so I guess it's possible," Ed responded. "Still, it's odd he'd not have his cell phone with him. He would have needed it in case Eric Klein tried to reach him or there was some sort of village emergency."

"We have a little time until the press conference starts. I'll run over and check and meet you back here as soon as I'm finished."

Several minutes later, she reported, "No luck, they weren't there."

Just then, Barb called on the intercom. "Elaine Morton from the *Silver Bay Times*, and Chad Burrows and his cameraman, Luke Granger, from WLCTV, are here for the press conference. Should I send them back?"

"Yes." She grimaced. "Might as well get this over with."

The tall, slim police chief stretched, and pulled her light brown hair into a ponytail, securing it with a rubber band she'd retrieved from the top drawer of her desk. After buttoning her navy-blue blazer over a tailored white shirt, she smoothed her khaki pants, and, when she spotted mud on her low brown boots, grabbed a tissue to clean them.

Within seconds, the three investigators greeted the reporters. The cameraman placed a small microphone on Carrie's jacket lapel, did a sound check, then gave her a thumbs up. Carrie faced the camera and announced that the mayor had died earlier that day from gunshot wounds, and the medical examiner had ruled his death a homicide. She introduced Ed and Brad and said they'd be working on the investigation and asked that anyone with information contact her or the two investigators as soon as possible. All tips would be treated with confidentiality.

Luke turned off the camera and removed the microphone. Carrie turned to the reporters.

"At this point, that's about as much I can tell you. We'll call or email you with updates as we have them."

Elaine, wearing jeans, black boots, and a blue down vest over a black sweater, tucked her short brown hair behind her ears and asked, "Can you tell us who found the body?"

"I can. University of Rochester students and their professor. They were supposed to meet the mayor for a tour of Freedom Hill."

"I might want to interview them. Could I get their contact information?"

"Eric Klein is the professor; I can give you his phone number, but I'm not going to give you the students' names. I've been informed they're traumatized from the experience."

"Carrie, you know I can get that information from the police report."

"Elaine, Brad's not including their names in his report; they had nothing to add that would have been pertinent to our investigation."

Chad Burrows, wearing a blue suit and tie, his short blond hair perfectly groomed, asked, "Any idea when the funeral will be?"

"When I spoke with Cheryl Butler several hours ago, she said Alex was to be cremated. I don't know if there will be a memorial service. I realize the death of our mayor is big news, still, I would appreciate your giving his family a little space. They deserve some privacy right now."

"Fair enough," Chad responded. Elaine nodded in concurrence.

"When will Janice Shaheen, the deputy mayor, be sworn in as mayor?" Elaine asked.

"I would imagine as soon as possible. The village board of trustees will make that decision; you'll have to speak with the president, Jed Cohen."

"Is he in today? What about Janice?"

"I have no idea. As you know, Village Hall is just across the parking lot. Perhaps your next stop can be a visit there. Now, please excuse me, we have a murder to solve."

The reporters left. Brad told Carrie he was going to his office to finish writing his report, and Ed drove home. Carrie sighed, put her head down on her desk and covered her face with her hands. She'd had extensive training in media relations but dealing with the press was one of her least favorite parts of her job. Sitting up, she took a sip of her now-cold coffee, shrugged her shoulders, stretched her neck muscles, and turned on her computer.

Chapter 10

Gretchen was asleep on her bed in the kitchen snoring lightly, a sound Ed found comforting and calming. She hadn't stirred when he entered the room, her hearing wasn't quite as acute as it used to be. Not wanting to startle her, he crouched next to her and gently rubbed the top of her head.

Her eyes opened, and when she recognized him, she wagged her tail, yawned, stretched into a downward dog position, leaned against him for more rubs then headed to the back door. He let her out, and in seconds she'd done her business and was scratching on the door to come inside. When she realized Ed had filled her dish with kibbles, she ran over to it and within seconds was licking the bowl clean.

"Want to go for a walk?" he asked as soon as she'd finished eating. The dog wagged her tail again and started turning around in circles, whimpering with excitement. Walks were one of the best things in life for Gretchen, after eating and belly rubs.

Ed retrieved her harness, leash, and a red quilted jacket from a hall tree in the mudroom and grabbed a couple of waste bags from the closet.

He'd just closed the front door when his phone rang. "Hi, Carrie. Can I call you back? I was just about to walk Gretchen."

"This won't take long, Ed. When can you meet tomorrow morning?"

"Whatever works for you is fine with me, my schedule's clear."

"How about 9:00 at Louise's?" She laughed. "I can never say no to a cup of her high-test coffee." She told Ed about Arturo's ear infection. "I spoke with his sitter. She said the antibiotic is starting to work, and the pain meds have kicked in. He seems to be doing better, but I can't foresee getting enough sleep until my children are grown."

"Annie and I know the challenges of raising small children when both parents have busy careers, Carrie. I hope tonight will be better, and you'll be able to get some rest. See you in the morning."

After placing the phone in his jacket pocket, Ed strolled with Gretchen to a beach a few blocks away from his house. Front yards along the route were carpet-thick with fallen leaves that swirled in the wind. A few maples and sumacs still bore color: their brilliant orange and fiery red a sharp contrast to the stark brown and grey landscape.

Sidewalks and roads were strewn with fallen ripe horse chestnuts; squirrels grabbing up those whose spiny shells had been cracked and broken open by passing motor vehicles. Ed smiled as he watched two entrepreneurial grey ones with reddish tails carry the rounded orbs away, their cheeks puffed out like blowfish.

During the summer, the beach was cleaned daily; now it was littered with rocks, pearly fresh-water shells, and small pieces of brown and grey driftwood. Sea gulls hopped about, scratching in the sand for freshwater mollusks; waves rolled lazily onto shore.

Gretchen hated water, except to drink it. She was stoic about baths because she had no choice; as much as she loved walking on the beach, she stayed far back from the water's edge. The slapping sound of the waves as they pounded upon the shore unnerved her.

Ed removed her leash so she could chase the gulls. He laughed when they flew upward, wings beating against the wind, in a mass to escape her. She turned and grinned at him, her big dark eyes shining. His heart swelled with love for this gentle, sweet dog who'd been a part of their family for more than a decade.

Several minutes later, she returned to his side, panting a bit, and wagging her tail. He affixed the leash to her harness and strolled along the sandy shore towards home.

Chapter 11

Carrie had a headache. She popped a couple of pain pills into her mouth and swallowed them with the stale coffee she'd poured from the machine in the lobby. She had tried cutting back on caffeinated beverages, but she was frequently exhausted and depended on the stimulant to give her a jolt of energy. She hoped the reporters would accurately report the facts and not harass Cheryl Butler or Eric Klein, but it was out of her hands.

Her phone rang; it was her husband, Matt, who worked as an emergency room doctor at the local hospital.

"Hi, honey. I heard about Alex Butler's death. Sad situation."

"News certainly travels fast in our little village, Matt. It's horribly sad and quite scary that someone could be murdered in broad daylight just a few miles outside the village." She paused. "Not that it hasn't happened before."

"When will you be home? You didn't get much sleep last night."

"Neither of us did, and my head's killing me. I want to speak with Mia before she starts her shift at 3:30; she's working nights until she finishes her master's degree in criminal justice at R.I.T. I don't have anything scheduled after that and unless something earth-shattering happens, I should be able to come home early."

"I'll pick up Arturo at the sitter's and Natasha from preschool at 4:30 so you can have some peace and quiet before the evening chaos starts. How about if instead of cooking, we keep things simple and order salad and a pizza from The Brewery?"

"That works for me."

Matt said, "Carrie, I'm concerned about you. You haven't felt well for ages."

"I'm not sure I completely shook off the postpartum depression after Arturo was born, Matt, plus I'm juggling a career with erratic hours along with family responsibilities. I don't know what to do about it.

"When I took this job, I was in heaven; this was my dream. Now that we have children, I'm not so sure. The mayor's death is really getting to me, and I expect my lack of sleep because of Arturo's ear infection isn't helping the situation."

"If you continue to feel depressed, perhaps you should consider scheduling a checkup and getting some counseling."

"I think I'll be okay once I can get a couple of good nights' sleep. I promise if I'm not feeling better in a couple weeks, I'll see our family doctor and make an appointment with a therapist. I don't want you to be responsible for more than your share of the household responsibilities or childrearing, Matt. You have a lot on your plate, too."

"When we married, Carrie, we pledged our love for better or for worse. This is a blip on the radar, and I'm here to help you with whatever you need."

"I love you," Carrie replied and hung up the phone.

At 3:30, Mia wrapped on Carrie's door.
"Come in, Mia."
'You wanted to see me?"
'Yes, you're patrolling solo this evening until 11:30, and I wanted to caution you to be careful and be on the lookout for suspicious activity. Alex's murder might have been a one-off, but we can't completely rule out that this might not be an isolated incident and the killer will strike again.

"If you see anything alarming, don't take chances; call the sheriff's office for back-up. As you know, they are on call when we need them. I'll be home all night, so if anything concerns you, please contact me on my cell phone instead of going through the dispatcher." She wrote her number on a sticky note.

Mia placed the note in a pocket, "Will do."

"Thanks, Mia. See you tomorrow. Hopefully, your evening will be uneventful."

Carrie ushered her patrolwoman out the door, grabbed her laptop and purse and locked the door behind her, taking a deep breath. She'd be in the safety and warmth of her home in ten minutes, praying that she could enjoy the evening with her family without interruptions.

Chapter 12

Ed sat in front of the fire ensconced in a large, leather recliner, nursing a glass of scotch, with Gretchen snuggled in beside him. He was listening to Edvard Grieg's *Peer Gynt, Suite #1*, "In the Hall of the Mountain King," when he heard the front door open.

Seconds later, Annie entered the living room, bent down to kiss her husband of more than 45 years, then nuzzled the dog. Gretchen looked up, sighed, then tucking her head into her small body, fell back asleep.

"Contented pair," she observed, smiling.

"I fed Gretchen and took her for a walk, now I'm enjoying the peace that precedes chaos. Might as well take advantage of it."

"You're already overwhelmed just thinking about investigating Alex's death, aren't you?"

He nodded. "I'm meeting Carrie and Brad at Louise's tomorrow morning at 9:00 to discuss how we're going to proceed.

"I have no idea what the techs found; I'm assuming we'll get a report within the next day or two; in the meantime, I'll check state and federal databases for recent shotgun purchases, although I know—excuse the terrible pun—that it's a long shot. The gun that killed him could have been purchased years ago, borrowed, or even stolen.

"Annie, each murder I've investigated over the past few years has had enough twists and turns to qualify as a segment of the game, *Twister*. I'm trying to stay optimistic and upbeat, still, these cases are never as easy to solve as I expect. How was the rest of your day?"

"It was okay. The high school students were understandably upset when they learned about Alex's murder, but they decided to stay for the tour. The news hit one of them, Billy Cooper, especially hard. He said

Alex and his father had been close friends since childhood, and the families spent a lot of time together."

She changed the subject. "It's been a busy year; I'll be glad when we close the museum to the public for a few months after Christmas. We have plenty to do this winter, including finalizing details for the opening celebration at Macyville. Our board will meet early in January to elect a new executive committee. Janice Shaheen will replace Alex as an ex-officio member."

"Is Suzanne going to continue as president?" Ed asked.

Suzanne Gordon, one of Annie's closest friends, had been elected president after their good friend Charles Merrill, suffering from ill health, had returned to Canada, where he was a citizen and had worked as a professor at the University of Toronto before retiring and relocating to Lighthouse Cove.

Originally from Jamaica, Suzanne ran the wellness center in the village and was married to Garrett Rosenfeld, a partner in a law firm in Rochester, where her parents ran a five-star rated Caribbean restaurant, Callaloo. The couple split their time between their cottage on the bay in Lighthouse Cove and a condo in the city.

"She can only serve two full terms but will remain on the board as immediate past president. I forgot to tell you she called yesterday and invited us to come to dinner at the cottage this Sunday evening. I don't have anything on my calendar other than volunteering that morning at the hospital. I haven't spent time with her for ages and would like to go."

"Me, too. Tell her we'll be there." He paused. "Can I pour you a glass of wine? How about some cheese and crackers?"

"That would be lovely, Ed; we can take our time and relax a bit. While you do that, I'll lower the temperature on the slow cooker to 'keep warm'. The stew should be fine until we're ready to eat."

After finishing their dinner, they placed the dishes in the dishwasher and let Gretchen out. When she came back inside, they moved into the family room where they sat quietly in matching leather chairs; Annie, knitting, and Ed, reading a biography of Ulysses S. Grant, Brahms' *Symphony # 2 in D Major* playing in the background. Gretchen crawled into her bed by the fireplace, the flames casting flickering shadows on the wall.

Thirty minutes later, Annie turned to her husband and said, "I thought knitting mittens for our grandchildren for Christmas would take my mind off Alex's murder, but it hasn't. I'm very sad, and I'm very weary."

"Of course you are. His death is not only a tragedy for the community, but also for you, personally. You and he worked together for months and became good friends. How about if I fix you a cup of chai and run a bubble bath for you?"

Annie smiled. "I'll take you up on your offer. Thank you."

Within several minutes, Ed escorted Annie up the stairs to their bathroom. The deep claw foot tub was filled with fragrant lavender-smelling bubbles, and on a stool next to the tub a steaming cup of sweet, creamy tea redolent with spices awaited her.

Before she got into the tub, Annie hugged her husband. "I always knew I made the right decision when I married you."

"It goes both ways, Annie. You've always been there for me when I've needed you, too. That's what a loving and enduring relationship is about."

Ed kissed the top of his wife's head. "I'm going downstairs to finish my chapter. Enjoy your bath."

Chapter 13

At 8:45 the next morning, Carrie grabbed her laptop from her office and walked down the hall to collect Brad before heading across the street to meet Ed. Barbara motioned her over to her desk.

"Janice Shaheen and her husband are here and want to speak with you. They're in the interview room."

"Can it wait? Brad and I are meeting with Ed in a few minutes at Bistro Louise."

"I don't think so. Janice is a bit hysterical. She thinks she killed Alex."

"What?"

Barbara sighed. "You should go talk with her."

Carrie shook her head and muttered, "Unbelievable. Barb, Ed's probably on his way to the Bistro and may even be there now waiting for us. Brad's in his office. Would you please call and let them know what's going on and ask that they join me in the interview room?"

"Sure thing."

The deputy mayor was sitting at a table sobbing, her husband, Nicholas, beside her. Carrie was confused. Janice and Alex had run against each other in a contentious race; after winning the election, he surprised everyone in the village by appointing her his deputy. She assumed they'd made their peace with one another; what motive would she have for killing him?

Janice took a few deep breaths. She was trembling; her husband placed his arm around her shoulders to calm her. Carrie said she'd be back in a minute, paid for two bottles of water in the vending machine in the lobby, and had just handed them to the couple when Brad appeared.

Thanking Carrie, Janice opened the bottle, took a few big gulps, then started explaining. Her father and brother took a day off work and went hunting together each November, and it continued even after her brother married and moved to Iowa. This year he couldn't make the trip to Lighthouse Cove because his wife had recently given birth to their first child; he didn't feel right about being away for several days. Her dad asked if she wanted to accompany him instead.

Although she had a full plate as deputy mayor, Janice felt bad that he and her brother would not be able to be together for their annual tradition. When she was younger, she occasionally tagged along with them but never really enjoyed it, although she'd learned how to use a gun. When her father said she could use her brother's, she decided to join him.

She learned the mayor was spending that day with college students and their professor and offered to ask her father to reschedule. Alex responded that it wasn't necessary, that there were few emergencies in the village this time of year; and that he'd carry his cell phone with him if anyone needed to reach him.

"What makes you think you killed him, and why did you wait until this morning to report it?" Carrie asked, skeptical that the deputy mayor was responsible for Alex's death.

Janice explained that she'd spotted a deer in her scope and shot at it, missing the first time, but certain she'd felled it with the second shot. She and her father searched, but when they couldn't find it, it became clear the deer was still alive.

Shortly after, her father bagged a deer. Her mother was in Iowa helping to care for the new baby, and after transporting the deer to the butcher for processing, she and her father went out for an early dinner; then went back to his house where they spent the evening together. She got home around 9:00.

"Didn't anyone contact you about Alex's death?"

"I had my cell phone with me, but there's hardly any reception in the woods. When I got back to my dad's house I found messages from Jed Cohen, Elaine Morton, and Nick. No one gave details about why they were calling, just asked that I call as soon as possible.

"Jed and I have been working on a grant application for a beach reclamation project, I thought that might be why he had called. I figured I could talk with him this morning. I had no idea why the reporter wanted to speak with me but decided that whatever it was could wait. I figured I'd find out what Nick wanted when I got home. He didn't indicate there was an emergency."

She looked at her husband. "As soon as I got home, he told me about Alex. I realized that's why Jed and the reporter had called. Jed and his husband have small children, and I thought it might be too late to call him back. I was too shocked and weary to call the reporter."

"How did you learn about Alex's death?" Carrie asked Nick.

He responded, "I took a break and went down to the cafeteria at work to get a cup of coffee and a donut, and while I was eating I checked the local news on my phone. I read about Alex's death and called Janice. As she explained, the call went to voicemail."

Janice said, "When we watched the 10:00 news last night and I learned more of the details, I was certain I'd killed Alex. I must have overshot my mark and instead of hitting the deer, the bullet went into the restricted area where he was waiting to meet the students.

"Please believe me; this was not premeditated. There was some animosity between us when we were running against each other during the mayoral campaign, but I really didn't expect to win, and then he asked if I would serve as deputy mayor. We became friends, he was a good man."

By now, Ed had entered the room.

Carrie said, "Hi, Ed. I'm assuming Barb explained why we're all here?"

Ed nodded and sat down next to Carrie.

"Sorry for interrupting, Janice," Carrie said. "Please continue."

"I know you have small children," she continued, "and I didn't want to bother you last night either, so when I told Nick I thought I was responsible for the mayor's death, we decided to wait until this morning for me to turn myself in. Neither of us slept a wink last night. I'm sick about what happened." She started crying again.

Carrie thought for a moment; then asked, "What type of gun do you use for hunting?"

"A Ruger American."

"I don't hunt. Is it a shotgun or a rifle?"

"It's a rifle."

"Excuse me a minute." Carrie left the interview room and called Mike Garfield.

Without preamble she asked, "You did say a shotgun killed Alex, right?"

"Yes. I know the difference between a shotgun slug and a bullet from a rifle. Why?"

"Long story, I'll fill you in later. Did the techs ever call you back and let you know the make and model of the gun that killed him?"

"As a matter of fact, I just hung up the phone with one of them and was just about to call you. Alex was killed with a Remington 870 12-gauge, the slugs matched that model. They didn't find suspicious prints anywhere; the blood was his, ditto for the scrapings I collected from under his fingernails. There was no sign of a struggle, and the bruising I found on the back of his head and his torso were from when he fell backwards onto some large rocks after he was shot.

"The techs found a few hair strands that weren't Alex's; they'll take samples from the Butlers to rule them out and see if the ones they found at the scene match any in the national DNA database. They found cigarette butts near his car, they'll check the database for those, too.

"My contact said there were lots of footprints, many were superimposed over others, and it was impossible to make impressions. Ditto for tire tracks. I'm afraid there's not much for you and your investigators to go on."

"That's unfortunate, but we'll deal with the hand we're given. Thanks so much, Mike. I'll talk with you soon."

A minute later, Carrie asked Janice if she happened to have brought the rifle with her.

"I did; I wanted to turn it in; I didn't think I'd be permitted past the reception area with it. It's in the back of our SUV."

"Where's your car?"

"In the parking lot at Village Hall, it's a white Chevy Blazer."

"May I have your keys?"

"I drove," Nick said. He reached into his pocket, took them out and handed them to Carrie who gave them to Brad. "Please check it out."

A few minutes later, the detective reappeared. "A Ruger American rifle is in the Blazer. It's recently been fired."

Carrie looked at Janice. "Three slugs from a shotgun—not bullets from a rifle—were pumped into Alex. You're in the clear."

Janice crumpled in relief, then started crying again.

Carrie waited until she composed herself. "Can you remember anything about yesterday morning that could help us? Did you see anything suspicious?"

"No, we parked in the White Birch lot, southeast of Freedom Hill, and crossed the road to the woods. We saw a few other hunters, that's all."

"What about your father? Might he remember something you haven't?"

A tablet with a pen next to it was lying on the table. Janice tore off a sheet and wrote down her father's name and contact information.

"I can't imagine he noticed anything, either, Carrie, but it's certainly worth giving him a call."

"Janice, I know how upsetting it must have been for you to think you killed the mayor. You were brave to come here," Carrie noted. "I appreciate it, and I'm glad it wasn't you."

Chapter 14

Carrie needed another coffee fix, and the investigators were hungry—none of them had eaten breakfast. The Bistro was crowded at that time of the morning, mostly with retirees who lingered over beverages and sweet rolls and caught up with the latest news. They found an empty table next to a window overlooking the lake.

Terri, their server, approached them with a scowl on her face and without a sound filled their coffee cups. She wore black leggings, black booties and a long-sleeved red tunic with the bistro's logo printed in white. When she noticed Brad, her scowl turned into a big smile, her eyes lighting up.

Questions came like a rapid-fire BB gun. "Each time I see the three of you together, it's not good news... I heard about the mayor's death... he was a decent guy and I voted for him.... It's scary that he was murdered... any idea who did it? You wouldn't be here unless you're investigating it.... Have you made any progress?"

Terri was a gossip and frequently in a snit when the information she sought wasn't easily obtained; Carrie decided to be straightforward and share as much as she could.

"Yes, Terri, the mayor was murdered yesterday. A University of Rochester professor and his students found the body at Freedom Hill. I can't give you any other details; we're just beginning to investigate."

"Well, that's too bad. There've been a lot of murders in this village over the past few years. What's happening around here?"

None of the investigators answered. Realizing she wasn't going to get additional information, Terri recited the specials.

She took Brad's order first: an egg-white omelet with a side of fruit and dry whole-grain toast. Ed ordered three eggs over easy, buttered whole-grain toast, a side of hash browns, orange juice. Carrie ordered a blueberry scone with a side of lemon curd and two slices of bacon. Their orders arrived quickly; as they ate, they discussed the case.

"Brad, if you don't mind, I think it would be more productive if I interview Cheryl by myself," Ed said. "She doesn't know you and if she has any ideas about who killed Alex, she might be more forthcoming if you're not present."

"I'm fine with that, Ed. I can use the time to wrap up a couple other cases. Carrie, you okay with this?"

The police chief nodded.

"I'll call her after we're finished here." Ed paused. "Has the press conference resulted in any leads?"

"Not so far; remember, it's early days."

"What's on your agenda for today?"

"I have a few things to catch up on that aren't related to the murder, then I'll call Mike to give him an update on what just happened with Janice and ask when he'll release Alex's body to the funeral home."

Audio #2 Abraham and Miranda Butler

Abraham Butler was born in Georgia in 1835, the son of a kitchen slave and the planter who owned her; three years later his 22-year-old mother died after giving birth to a second child, Betsey. An attractive young man with the green eyes of his father, Abraham was sold in 1843 as a house slave to a wealthy Maryland banker and educated alongside his master's children.

In 1848, with a crisis of conscience, his master freed Abraham and sent him to Philadelphia where he became the ward of a Quaker cousin, Ephraim Butler, and his wife, Beatrice. The parents of Miranda, who was a year younger, the couple treated the intelligent young man like the son they'd never had.

The two young people became inseparable, and after a time their friendship turned to romantic love; in 1855 they decided to wed. But a law passed in Pennsylvania in 1780 prohibited marriage between the two races and they were quickly dispatched by their elders to Macyville, where Ephraim's abolitionist brother lived.

Within a week of their arrival, they recited their vows before the community and set up housekeeping in a small cottage at the settlement. Abraham obtained work as a teacher at the settlement school and later became its headmaster; Miranda arranged passage to Canada for fleeing slaves, and after the Civil War ended, she helped repatriate those who wished to return.

Their first child, Abigail, was born in 1856; their second, Dollie, in 1858; and in 1860, the Butlers welcomed a third child, whom they named Alex. In 1862, Miranda's parents sold their home and belongings in Philadelphia and relocated to Macyville to be nearer their family.

Abraham and Miranda lived long and healthy lives, raised their children and watched them prosper, and experienced the joys of welcoming grandchildren and great-grandchildren to the family. Abraham died in 1909, Miranda in 1913. Their descendants remained in the area, settling in nearby Lighthouse Cove after World War I.

Chapter 15

After breakfast the next morning, Ed called Cheryl Butler who said the medical examiner had contacted her to let her know that Alex's body had been released to the funeral home. Her children were there now with her sister, arranging for his cremation. She agreed to speak with him before they returned home.

Half an hour later, Ed pulled into a parking space in front of the Butler house. Located high on a hill three miles south of Lighthouse Cove, the sprawling Mediterranean-style home was painted cream, with sage-green trim. A silver-gray minivan was parked under an attached *port cochere* on the right. The broad front yard, with evergreens pruned in a variety of shapes and sizes along the tall front windows, was bisected by a tan brick sidewalk that led up three semi-circular steps to a large front porch and an ochre-colored door.

He rang the doorbell, and within seconds, the grieving woman, barefooted and wearing matching dark blue sweatpants and sweatshirt, ushered him into the kitchen, a pleasant, bright room occupying the back of the house. Ed accepted a glass of water and after brewing a cup of tea for herself, Cheryl sat down next to him.

"I'm not sure what more I can tell you that I didn't tell Carrie, Ed. I looked everywhere and not only is Alex's cell phone missing, but I also couldn't find his computer or USB drive. He spent months working on the Macyville project, and it appears all his recent research has disappeared. I'm sick about it."

"Of course you are. Carrie said you told her Alex wanted to speak with you about something when you got home from your conference but wouldn't tell you what it was about over the phone. She said you don't believe it had anything to do with his murder, but is it possible he didn't want to alarm you and didn't want to say anything to you until you could speak person?"

"I don't know." Cheryl thought for a minute. "Maybe. Did you know Alex was working with a genealogist and *FindYourRoots.com* to locate other living descendants of the Butler, Cooper, and Ward families so he and Annie could invite them to the Macyville grand opening?"

"Yes."

"He was making progress. Not surprisingly, some are Black; some are white; others, mixed race.

"Most of the people Alex contacted were delighted with the news and eager to participate, but one man was not receptive. It appears he and Alex are distant relatives, but the man thought Alex was scamming him and insisted he had no ancestors who'd been enslaved or Black.

"He threatened Alex with legal reprisal or worse if he continued to contact him and asked to be removed from the list. As disappointed as he was, Alex apologized and said he'd delete his information. What if the man didn't believe him and killed Alex to keep secret his ancestry? Unfortunately, I don't think Alex ever told me his name or where he lived. If he did, I don't remember it."

"Is it possible he confided in someone besides you about the conversation?"

"He plays poker every week with friends from childhood. Alex and I shared everything, but I suppose it's possible he might have spoken with one of them." She told Ed about the men and sent him a text with their contact information.

Chris Bayley was an FBI agent who worked from home but was assigned to the Buffalo field office; Greg Cooper, the father of the student who toured the exhibit with his class the day before, owned the local hardware store; Larry Monroe was an apple farmer; Dave

Stanford, a dentist. Vic Sloan owned a diner in Williamson.

"Thanks. I'll set up interviews. Can you think of anything else that might help with the investigation?"

At first Cheryl shook her head, then she had an 'aha' moment. "I just remembered something, but I really can't imagine he'd kill Alex, although what happened was scary and upsetting at the time."

"If there's someone you think we should interview, you need to tell me."

"It's embarrassing. I met a man—another principal—at the same conference in Albany last year…but no, he couldn't be involved…"

"Cheryl, if there's even a remote possibility that he killed Alex, we need to schedule an interview with him."

She started to cry. Ed sat patiently for a few minutes until she composed herself. Then she explained.

Chapter 16

As Cheryl had mentioned to Carrie, she'd been away at an annual conference for a few days and had returned the morning of Alex's murder. The previous year she and three others had sat on a panel to present information about their schools' innovative math programs. One of them, Kurt Appleby, was the intermediate school principal with the Baldwinsville School District, located about an hour southeast of Lighthouse Cove.

The conference resulted in formation of a regional task force to establish joint professional development programs for intermediate schools in districts within a certain geographical area. She and Kurt were invited to serve on that task force and agreed to work together on a specific piece of the project.

They met a few times and after a while, Cheryl sensed that he was attracted to her; he was giving out signals that he wanted to pursue a personal relationship. He was a widower, she realized he was vulnerable, and she told him that she hoped she hadn't inadvertently encouraged him as she was happily married.

"He was angry with me, Ed; he said he believed I *had* led him on. I was flabbergasted. I assure you I have no idea why he believed that. I apologized again, and he appeared to accept that we could never be more than acquaintances.

"I hoped that would be the end of it, but it wasn't. He sent me flowers at work; I refused them. He sent inappropriate emails until I blocked him. Then he started calling and leaving messages and texting me on my cell phone. I blocked his phone number and was considering going to the police but had second thoughts. I didn't want to ruin his career; instead, I withdrew from the task force, citing family concerns.

"Normally I fight my own battles; what I was doing didn't seem to be working. I told Alex what was happening, and we decided it might be more effective if he called Kurt, hoping he'd disappear when he learned I was telling the truth about my marriage."

"How did he react when Alex called him?" Ed asked.

"Alex said he seemed contrite, apologized, and promised not to contact me again. And he didn't. Now I'm wondering if he was only pretending to appease my husband."

"Was he at the conference this year? If so, how did he act towards you?"

"No, he wasn't." She took a deep breath. "He must have known I'd be there; a list of attendees is published and sent to all the intermediate school principals in New York. Maybe he decided to kill Alex while I was at the conference.

"A couple months ago, there was an article in *Life in the Finger Lakes* magazine about the work Alex was doing with the historical society. It gave details about the field trip with the university students and mentioned that others were welcome to join the group. Even though Kurt lives in Baldwinsville, the magazine covers the entire region and it's possible he read the article.

"He may have saved Alex's phone number from when they spoke. His undergraduate degree is in history; maybe he called him to request they meet at Freedom Hill before the field trip, indicating that while he was interested in taking the tour, the timing wouldn't work because of his schedule.

"Kurt never seemed unhinged to me, just lonely, but what if he's not who he appeared to be? I've read that sociopaths can be very convincing liars, and with Alex out of the way, perhaps he believed he'd have a chance with me."

"It would explain the missing cellphone, but what about his USB drive and computer?"

"The only thing on the USB drive was the audio description Alex was to bring to Annie, but he wouldn't have known that. He might have taken it and the laptop just in case there was incriminating information in them.

"If he killed my husband, how will I ever forgive myself?" Cheryl started crying again.

"This isn't your fault, Cheryl. It sounds to me like you did everything in your power to discourage Appleby. It's also possible that Appleby didn't attend the conference for a different reason, and he had nothing to do with Alex's murder. Do you happen to know if he hunts?" Ed asked.

"No. Until he tried to make it personal, we never talked about anything other than the work we were doing on the task force."

"My instincts are telling me he's not Alex's killer. I think whoever murdered him had a much more sinister reason for wanting him dead. Still, I'll follow up on the lead."

Ed heard voices coming from the living room. Cheryl's children and her sister had returned and rushed into the kitchen, surrounded her, and looked quizzically at Ed.

He introduced himself and said he was investigating their father's death and wanted to come by to speak with their mother and express his condolences. "Thank you for seeing me, Cheryl."

She rose from her chair and hugged him. He looked at her three children and said, "Please know how sorry I am for your loss."

Chapter 17

Ed stopped at the police station to report to Carrie on his conversation with Cheryl.

"Before I call to schedule an interview with Kurt Appleby, can you do a background check on him?"

"Sure, what are you looking for?"

"DUIs, speeding, parking tickets. I expect you'll not find much; he'd not be a school administrator if he's been in previous trouble with the law."

"I'll have that information to you within an hour, Ed. Anything else?"

"Yes, check to see if he's purchased a shotgun recently or if he has a hunting license."

"I'll call you as soon as I have the report. Have you thought about how you're going to get him to agree to speak with you?"

"I have. I've done some consulting for the police department in Baldwinsville, and Jim Parsons, the chief there, is a friend. I'll call him and see how he wants to handle this, but I don't think he'll have a problem with my speaking directly with Appleby without his being present.

"After that, I'll schedule an appointment with the principal. I'll say I'm working on a case with the police department, I won't tell him which one, and indicate it would be helpful if I could talk with him about it. I've learned that being vague is sometimes the best strategy." He grinned.

"If I get a sense Appleby killed Alex or might have hired someone to do it for him, I'll call Jim, and we'll bring him in as a person of interest, but I don't think that's going to happen. My gut is telling me he's not our killer. I'm only interviewing him to reassure Cheryl and because we can't leave any stones unturned."

Ed went home and called the Baldwinsville police chief who, after hearing his plan, said he appreciated the heads up, but as Ed had surmised, didn't need to be present for the interview.

He ended the call, and his phone rang again. It was Carrie.

"I just emailed you Appleby's report. He's clean. He has no criminal record, although he did get a speeding ticket several years ago for going 35 in a 25-mile-an-hour zone. No DUIs, no recent gun purchases or hunting license, although, as we've already discussed, whomever killed Alex could have borrowed or stolen the gun."

"Thanks, Carrie. I'm hoping to be able to make an appointment with him for today."

When Ed called the Baldwinsville School District and asked to speak with Kurt Appleby, his administrative assistant, Rick Kaufmann, answered. Ed explained the purpose for his call and said he'd hoped they could schedule a meeting as soon as possible.

Kaufmann responded that Appleby had returned that morning from several days leave. He wasn't sure of his schedule but knew the principal had a backlog of work to catch up on. He said he'd see what he could do, then put Ed on hold.

Ed thought it interesting that the principal had been away during the time of Alex's murder, but there could be a multitude of reasons for it.

In a couple minutes, Rick said that Dr. Appleby had an opening at 3:00 that day. Ed thanked him, indicating that the meeting wouldn't last long, and the call ended. Ed called the Baldwinsville police chief with an update and looked at his watch. It was just after noon, and he had an hour's drive to the school. He'd have plenty of time to get there.

Chapter 18

At a few minutes to 3:00, Ed pulled into a spot in the parking lot at Baldwinsville Intermediate School, walked into the building, showed a guard his driver's license and police credentials, and was escorted to Appleby's office.

A broad smile on his face, Rick Kaufmann greeted him. Getting up from his desk, he rapped on the principal's door.

"Your 3:00 is here," he announced.

"Come in, come in." The principal stood up from behind his desk, walked over to Ed and shook his hand; then he walked past him to shut the door for privacy. He appeared to be in his mid-50s, was about Ed's height with broad shoulders, a shock of short, dark brown hair parted on one side and candid brown eyes. Ed took out his credentials and showed them to the principal.

Appleby was wearing navy wool slacks, a light blue oxford cloth shirt, and a red and blue striped tie. A dark blue tweed sport coat hung on a coat tree to the right of the door. Ed noticed he was wearing a wedding ring and recalled Cheryl saying he'd been widowed and figured he was still grieving and hadn't yet emotionally been able to remove it.

His desk faced the door; behind it, from floor to ceiling, were bookcases jammed tightly with reference books, manuals, and professional publications. Academic degrees were framed and hung on a wall beside a window facing west. Ed noticed a photo of a young couple with a baby sitting on a credenza along the opposite wall. Next to it was a photo of Appleby with his arm around a slender, smiling blond woman, sailboats framing the background.

"That's my daughter, Jenna, and her family," Appleby offered, holding up the photo of the couple with the baby. "The baby is almost one now." Then he became somber. "I wish my wife were here. She died of cancer before the baby was born."

"I'm sorry for your loss." Ed didn't mention the other photo, expecting it would bring up sad memories.

Motioning for Ed to sit, Appleby said, "I believe you told Rick that you're working with our police department on a case, and I might be able to help you with your investigation. Does it have anything to do with one of our teachers or students?"

"I apologize for the subterfuge; I didn't think you'd agree to meet with me if I told you the real reason for my call. I'm not working with your police department; I'm working with the Lighthouse Cove police department, investigating the death of Alex Butler, who was shot to death yesterday morning. Would you happen to know anything about that?"

Appleby gasped. "That's just terrible. I'm shocked; I had no idea. You think....Oh my, you think I murdered him, don't you? Cheryl must have spoken with you."

"Cheryl said you and she had a history and that you weren't present at a conference you normally attend this time of year. Your assistant said you'd been away for a few days. After learning that she'd be at the conference, did you take off some time to kill her husband?"

"No, of course not. I would never do something so heinous. This is all a terrible mistake. I can explain."

He reiterated to Ed what Cheryl had told him. "I had been recently widowed when Cheryl and I first met at the conference in Albany. My wife died a month after she was diagnosed with pancreatic cancer, and I was extremely needy and in shock. I expect Cheryl mentioned that we were asked to serve on a task force together. I was vulnerable at the time and attracted to her.

"She wore a wedding ring, but so did I, and I wondered if she were widowed, too. When she said she was married, I hoped maybe the marriage was unhappy, she disabused me of that quickly.

"I didn't want to believe her. I really liked her and admit it was hard for me to take no for an answer. I acted foolishly. I called her repeatedly, emailed her and sent flowers which she refused. She resigned from the task force, and then her husband called and in no uncertain terms told me to back off."

He rubbed his eyes, and continued, "I can't believe what a jerk I was. Cheryl did nothing to encourage me. I missed my wife so much, all I wanted was to jump into another relationship quickly to assuage the pain.

"I joined a grief support group and found solace in attending the weekly sessions and after a while became friendly with one of the women who, like me, had lost her spouse to cancer. We began to date."

He smiled. "Her name is Sharon Dillard; she's a travel agent. We got married last week." He picked up the photo on his desk and showed it to Ed.

"You asked why I didn't attend the conference? We took a brief wedding trip to the Thousand Islands, stayed at a beautiful inn in Clayton, and just got back last night."

He reached into the pocket of his slacks and pulled out a bunch of papers from his wallet. "Here, take these. They're the gas, hotel, and food receipts from our trip."

Ed looked through them and after several seconds nodded and placed them back on Appleby's desk.

"Mr. DeCleryk, my first wife was terrified of guns and opposed to hunting. I've never owned a gun in my life."

As disappointed as he was in not finding Alex Butler's killer, Ed was relieved that it wasn't the principal, an affable man who'd suffered a horrible loss and acted foolishly as the result of his grief.

Ed rose from his chair. "Thank you for speaking with me. I truly hope you and your new wife will be happy."

Appleby had a wry smile on his face. "Kind of ironic, isn't it, that at one time I truly believed Cheryl and I would be perfect for each other. Now that she's available, I'm happily remarried and realize we wouldn't have been in the least bit suited. Please tell her how terribly sorry I am for her loss and how much I regret that my actions distressed her and her husband."

The two men shook hands and Ed quietly let himself out, smiling at Rick, who was texting on his phone as he passed.

Chapter 19

"Well, that's another suspect off our list," Carrie remarked as she and Ed were sitting in her office drinking coffee an hour later. "I've learned since working with you that solving a murder case is never as easy as it appears on TV or in the movies. While I always hope we'll be able to settle a case quickly, I know it could take months."

"I'll call Cheryl tomorrow morning with an update rather than bothering her now," said Ed. "Before I left her house this morning, she said she was expecting a visit from some of her friends who were bringing dinner to her and her family tonight. I'm sure she'll be relieved that Appleby didn't kill Alex and happy he's found someone else."

"What are your plans for the rest of the day?"

"I'm going to go home to screen state databases for gun purchases, and, if I have time, I'll call Alex's friends to schedule a group interview. Annie and I are meeting our friends, Eve and Henri Beauvoir, for dinner tonight at The Brewery. A bluegrass group we enjoy will be performing."

Carrie groaned. "I'm envious. I can't recall the last time Matt and I had a date night, and because of my erratic schedule, even if we could, it would be hard to get a sitter at the last minute."

Ed had an idea, and after he returned home, he called Annie.

Several minutes later he dialed the police chief's number and when she answered said, "Carrie, I spoke with Annie, and we'd be happy to watch Natasha and Arturo this weekend, if it works for you and Matt."

"That's so kind, Ed. I'll call Matt to see what his plans are and get back to you."

A few minutes later, Ed answered his phone. "Hi, Ed, it's Carrie. We gratefully accept your offer, but Matt and I are so exhausted at night, watching the children during the day might be better for us. Would this Saturday afternoon work?"

"I'll check with Annie, but I think Saturday is free."

Changing the subject, he asked, "Will the conference room be available for the interviews with Alex's friends? If not, I can probably arrange to use the boardroom at Village Hall."

"There's nothing scheduled for the foreseeable future. Once you know the day and time, could you please call me with details? I'd like to sit in and will ask Brad to join us."

"Will do."

Chapter 20

Annie had no plans for Saturday afternoon. Ed texted Carrie with a thumbs up emoji and a message asking her to let him know what time she wanted them to arrive.

He let Gretchen out and fed her, then brewed himself a cup of tea and went into his study. The wind had picked up, and he could hear the waves crashing on the rocks at the base of the bluff beneath his home. Gretchen ambled in and curled up in a ball on one of her many beds placed in rooms throughout the house, her favorite stuffed blue bunny under her neck like a pillow.

Logging into his computer, he opened the state gun registry website, typed in his username and password, browsed for a few minutes, and learned that three people living in the area had recently purchased shotguns. He wrote down their contact information and called them, pleased when each person answered, and he didn't have to leave a message.

The first two were hunters. One worked for the county maintenance department; the other was a business owner. The third, a young woman who didn't hunt, was the director of the leadership program for the Rochester Chamber of Commerce and was taking night courses at Saint John Fisher College for an MBA. She volunteered that she'd purchased the gun as a surprise gift for an uncle because he'd said he had been thinking about buying a new one, but when she spoke with him several days later, he said he changed his mind, and she decided to return it.

There didn't seem to be any link to the mayor, and their alibis had quickly checked out. He made a list of questions for Alex's poker buddies, and then, when he finished, picked up the phone and called each of them. Expressing dismay and sadness over their friend's death and a willingness to help in any way they could, they agreed to meet at the station the next morning at 10:00.

He called Carrie.

"Oh, hi, Ed. I was just about to call you. Matt and I are wondering if it would be okay if we brought the kids to your house instead of you coming to ours. We'd like to go to the mall and shop; then if the weather cooperates, come back to our house, light a fire in the fire pit and have a romantic lunch at home."

"Carrie, you have such a fabulous view of the lake and the bay, an afternoon at home sounds perfect. We still have a crib and highchair from when our grandchildren were babies, so we're pretty well set. We'll expect you late morning."

Shortly before Natasha was born, Carrie and Matt had purchased a small three-bedroom cottage south of the village, across Silver Bay where homes perched on cantilevered hillsides with spectacular views of the water.

She sighed. "I'm looking forward to being with my husband without our children for a few hours. Sorry, I interrupted you. Why were you calling?"

Ed summarized his conversations with the three people who had recently purchased guns and let Carrie know that he'd scheduled interviews with Alex's friends for the next morning.

Chapter 21

Dressed in warm outerwear and holding hands, Ed and Annie, walked silently to The Brewery to meet their friends. Light snow mixed with a bit of freezing rain crunched beneath their feet and sparkled like prismed crystals under the tall, Victorian gas lamps that illuminated the streets.

The Beauvoirs, arriving first, had secured a round oak table at a window overlooking the water near the corner fireplace where applewood logs burned their sweet, smoky scent and warmed the room with steady flames. Henri had already ordered their drinks: a martini for himself, a Chardonnay for Eve, scotch for Ed, and Cabernet Sauvignon for Annie.

They made small talk for several minutes, then Eve announced that she and Henri were planning to sell their house on White Pelican Island and move back to the village.

"Why?" Annie asked. "I thought you loved it there." The island was situated on the southeastern side of the bay and accessed by a two-lane bridge. One end was a sanctuary for rare white pelicans that spent part of the winter and spring in upstate New York.

"Our house is way too large for us," Eve responded, "and our kids are scattered throughout the country, and as we're getting older, it's more and more difficult for us to climb those rickety steps that lead from our backyard down the hill to our boathouse."

Henri chimed in, "We're just in the planning stages right now; ideally we'd like a two-bedroom cottage where we could walk to the shops and restaurants in the village."

Ed asked, "What are you going to do with your boat?"

"We've already arranged to keep it at Harvey's Marina. We can rent a slip and off-season we'll store the boat in their high-and-dry facility."

"We'd love if you lived closer," Annie said. "We'll keep our eyes open and call you if we see anything for sale that might suit you."

"There's no hurry; we've just started to think about it," Eve replied.

Several minutes later, after perusing the menu and ordering their meals—the meatloaf special for the men and the perch dinners for the women—the couples settled in to listen to the happy bluegrass tunes of The Bay Boys.

By the time the DeCleryks began their walk home, the snow and rain had stopped, clouds had cleared, and the inky blue sky sparkled with a myriad of stars that winked and blinked above them. They agreed the evening had been perfect, and that they were pleased to have spent time with their friends, talking about subjects not related to Alex Butler's murder.

Chapter 22

The next morning Ed called Cheryl Butler. As he expected, she was relieved that Kurt Appleby was in the clear and pleased he'd remarried.

"I liked him until everything started going sideways," she said. "I truly hope he'll be happy."

"How are you holding up, Cheryl?"

She replied that her sister was providing as much emotional support as possible; her children, Alex's parents, and his sister were struggling. It was difficult for her to comfort them, given her own pain.

She was having trouble sleeping. The bedroom she'd shared with Alex made her acutely aware of her loss when she laid her head on the pillow next to where he had lain his for so many years.

"I can't imagine losing Annie in such a tragic way, Cheryl," Ed responded. "What an awful ordeal for you and your family."

"Last night was terrible, Ed. It was 1:00 a.m., the rest of my family was asleep, and I wandered into Alex's study." She started crying. "I so wanted to feel a connection with him, hoping to find a measure of comfort being near his things."

She'd touched the books on his bookshelves, sat at his desk, and opened the album of photos from their many family trips. She'd smiled when she saw them, then realized that there would be no more trips with Alex, ever. A wing chair sat in a corner of the room. She curled up into it and pulled a woolen throw over her body. She sat like that, crying quietly, hoping no one would hear her, until dawn.

"My only solace is that when I look at my children, I see Alex in them. If not for them, I don't know how I would manage to go on. He'll be cremated tomorrow morning. I'm dreading it."

Chapter 23

That same morning, shortly after she arrived at work, Carrie learned that two unlocked cars sitting in driveways two blocks from the historical society had been broken into the night before. The vandals had attempted to break into a third, then ran away when motion sensor lights turned on in the driveway.

Change drawers had been emptied with coins spilled onto the seats and, in one case, the burglars had opened the trunk, although it appeared nothing had been stolen.

She asked Brad to speak with the victims. He was disappointed that he wouldn't be able to sit in on the interview with Alex's childhood friends; Carrie promised an update as soon as he returned.

The men sat at a round table in the conference room, their mood somber. Chris Bayley nervously drummed his fingers on the table, Larry Monroe jiggled his right foot, Dave Stanford stared into the room, Vic Sloan looked down at his knees, and Greg Cooper clenched and unclenched his fists. The men wore blazers or sweaters over collared shirts; two wore jeans; the others, khakis.

Earlier, Carrie had asked Ed to take the lead on the questioning, and as he began, he sighed. "I can only begin to imagine how difficult this must be for all of you. Some of you may recall that my childhood friend, George Wright, was murdered 18 months ago. I don't think you ever get over something like that."

Greg spoke first. "It's horrible. I wake up each morning thinking about Alex and remembering how he died. Do you know that our poker games started when we were in high school?

"We played for peanuts, and I literally mean peanuts, and after we finished playing, we shelled and ate them and drank Cokes. The games stopped when we graduated, some of us went off to college and others to the military. We resumed our weekly poker night when we all moved back to Lighthouse Cove as adults. We still play for peanuts; now instead of Cokes, we drink beer."

The others laughed uneasily.

"If we continue our weekly tradition, it won't be the same," Vic reflected.

The others remained silent.

Then, to break the silence, Dave said, "We want to help you find Alex's killer; I just don't know what we can tell you."

Ed asked, "For starters, what about Alex's recent state of mind? Was anything bothering him? Did he seem to be acting differently? Cheryl said he'd been preoccupied lately. Any idea why?"

"We had our usual weekly poker game at my house the night before he was killed. Alex typically is the first one to leave; he allows himself only one beer. With Cheryl away at a conference, he stayed a little longer and had a second," Greg answered.

Dave responded, "He was more quiet than usual, and when I asked if everything was okay, he said he'd learned something recently that he couldn't share with us before telling Cheryl. Larry asked if he were having health problems; he said that he wasn't and changed the subject."

"After he had that second beer, he got up to leave," Richard answered, and turned to Chris. "He wanted to talk with you about something. You and he walked out together."

"That's right, you did," replied Greg, who bore an uncanny resemblance to his departed friend, including the green eyes. Ed, looking closely at the man, mentioned it.

"I know; we get that a lot," he responded, using present tense. "We've been best friends since middle school, maybe our looks rubbed off on each other."

He smiled, "we told people we were brothers from another mother; it always made them laugh. We're not related; it's just a coincidence."

"Interesting," Ed remarked, tucking the information away in his head. He turned to Chris, "What was it he wanted to speak with you about?"

Chris glanced at his watch, stared into space for a second as though thinking about how he wanted to answer, and said, "His son, Daniel, is a computer science major at SUNY Buffalo, and he asked if the Bureau is hiring interns for the summer at our field office there. I offered to check into it and said I'd get back to him within a few days.

"He was one of my closest friends, and now he's dead."

The five men looked at Ed and Carrie expectantly.

"This is just routine, and I hope not too disturbing; we need to know your whereabouts the morning he was killed," Ed stated.

No one seemed to take offense. Dave, the dentist, had been seeing patients, his receptionist and dental hygienist would vouch for him. Greg said his hardware store had opened at 7:00 a.m. and his employees would verify he was there. Vic had been at his diner since 6:00 a.m. getting ready for the breakfast crowd and had stayed until mid-afternoon.

After a successful harvest, Larry and his farm manager, Miguel, had hosted a celebration breakfast for his workers, many of whom were seasonal and about to depart for their homes in Mexico. He had no problem with Ed calling Miguel or his wife, Sofia, who had helped to prepare the breakfast.

Chris said, "I worked from home. I called my bureau chief about 10:00, it was my first call of the day. I think I still have the call log on my phone." He pulled it out, tapped on the phone icon and scrolled to recent calls.

He turned his screen to Ed. "You're welcome to contact her; she'll confirm our conversation." He grabbed a piece of paper and a pen from the table and wrote the information down. "Here's her phone number."

The man seemed genuinely sad about Alex's death. Ed had no reason to believe he was lying; still, his instincts told him Bayley was withholding information and wondered if Alex wanted to speak with him for a very different reason, one he couldn't share with the others.

Ed asked, "Do any of you own a gun?"

All the men raised their hands.

"For hunting?"

Dave answered. "We used to hunt together; as we got older, most of us lost interest, so now when we shoot, it's mostly at the gun club for target practice."

Greg volunteered, "I still hunt with my son, Billy. We haven't gone out yet this season."

"Thank you. Is there anything else any of you can think of that would help us find Alex's killer?" Ed asked.

The men were quiet for a few seconds, then Chris said, "Jill."

"Jill," Greg replied. "Of course."

Ed asked, "Who's Jill?"

Chris responded, "Alex was married once before; her name was Jill Clark. The marriage didn't last long, and Alex was the one who filed for the divorce; she was enraged about it. She married a man named Dan Spencer several years later.

"I bumped into her at the checkout counter at Lattimore's Pharmacy a few years after she and Alex split when she was visiting her parents. That was before she married Dan. We spoke briefly. She asked lots of personal questions about Alex and Cheryl and brought up the divorce. She sounded bitter.

"Fortunately, I was ahead of her in line and able to pay the cashier and get out of there before she could pummel me with more questions."

Richard interjected, "She and Dan go to our church. He's pleasant and polite, and they seem happy enough, but you never know what goes on behind closed doors."

Ed decided his next step would be to obtain Jill Spencer's contact information and schedule an interview with her.

Chapter 24

"I believe them," Carrie said to Ed after they left, "but just to make sure they're telling the truth, I'll have Brad confirm their alibis."

"Good idea." He paused. "Chris is withholding information, and I'm wondering if it's related to the conversation he and Alex had when they left the poker game. I want to interview him again."

"Without the others?"

"Yes, he may be more forthcoming if they're not with him."

"I had the same feeling. I'd like to sit in on that interview with Brad. Do you want to call Chris or shall I?" Carrie responded.

"Let's wait until after I interview Jill Spencer, then we can decide how to proceed."

He asked Carrie to get the woman's contact info, run a background check and see if there were guns registered in her or her husband's name.

Just as Ed was leaving, Brad strolled into her office.

"Peter VanDecker, one of the burglary victims, gave this to me, let's look at what's on it." He handed Carrie a USB drive. "The cameras from his security system picked it up."

Carrie turned on her computer, inserted the drive into a USB port and opened it. Three young men, wearing jeans and hoodies, were observed walking up the driveway. When the motion sensor lights turned on, they ran away; the video camera had picked up two of them.

"Peter showed it to his family. His son, Randy, who is a freshman at the high school, recognized them, their names are Dillon Seibert and Travis Green. He doesn't hang out with them, they're juniors."

"They're probably in school right now," Carrie noted. "What's your next step?"

"I'm going to go over to the high school and see if the principal will allow me to question them. Hopefully, they'll each give the other one up and identify the third. None of the families wants to press charges since nothing was taken; still, there should be consequences to their actions.

"I knew you were busy interviewing the mayor's friends and didn't think you'd have a problem if I called the county sheriff's office to ask if someone there would be willing to run a background check on the two boys. An undersheriff got back to me quickly. There aren't any police complaints for either of them, neither has been in trouble with the law; they're honor roll students. I'm hoping this is an isolated incident, just boys doing something stupid on a dare."

Chapter 25

Fifteen minutes later, after showing his credentials to the school security guard, Brad was escorted to the principal's office. He explained the reason for his visit, and she informed him that because the two boys were minors, parental permission was required for him to interview them; if they refused, he would have to wait until they could be present.

The parents agreed to the interviews, indicating that if their sons were involved in the vandalism, they would support whatever consequences were meted out to them for their actions.

"They gave him up," Brad said, standing in Carrie's doorway an hour later.

"Who gave whom up? What are you talking about?" Carrie asked.

"The two boys gave up the third. You won't believe who it is."

"I'm waiting with baited breath," Carrie smiled. "Don't tease me."

"Billy Cooper. Greg's son."

"We just finished interviewing him with Alex's other friends. He seems like a stand-up guy, from what I've heard they're a good family. Has he been called?"

"He has, we needed parental permission to interview the boys."

"How did he react?"

"He was angry and embarrassed. He said he and his wife have not raised their son to be disrespectful of others or their property. He wasn't trying to excuse his son's behavior but wondered, because Billy's never been in trouble before, if Alex's murder might have something to do with it. He said Billy has been quite upset; he seems to be holding on to his grief rather than talking about it to his parents. Anyway, Greg and his wife, Laura, will back up whatever punishment we decide with additional disciplinary action."

"How did you get the other two to give him up?" Carrie asked.

Brad grinned. "I asked them how they would feel if they were serving time in prison while he was out partying and going to football games."

"Brad," Carrie admonished. "These boys aren't going to go to jail for this crime."

He smirked. "I know. I didn't tell them they were going to jail, Carrie, I just asked them how they would feel about it. That was enough for them to finger him."

Carrie laughed. "Well, whatever it takes, I guess. Did they say why they did it?"

"Yes. As I suspected, it was on a dare. They hatched the plan at lunch one day. Billy was the ringleader."

Brad grinned and cocked an eyebrow. "As I fully understand from my own experiences, teenaged boys' brains are not fully developed. They can be quite impulsive and do things they don't think about and come to regret later."

"I *am* curious about something. How did they ever manage to get out of their houses without their parents knowing?"

"I asked that question. They waited until their families were asleep and just before midnight snuck out and rode their bikes to Sunset Park, the pocket park at the northern end of Lakeview St. It's a few blocks from where they all live, and a perfect location for their crime spree." Brad laughed.

"The homes on either side of the park are vacant this time of year; the owners spend their winters in Florida. There's an empty lot across the street on one corner, and on the other, the house is also vacant; it was sold this summer and the new owners are having it renovated before they move in. They planned well, knowing no one would be around to observe their shenanigans."

"Clever. How did they choose the homes to vandalize?"

"They rode their bikes south down Lakeview searching for cars parked in driveways between streetlights. As luck would have it, they found three in a row.

"What they didn't count on was that the VanDecker family had a security system installed with motion sensors on the garage. When the lights blinked on, they got on their bikes and rode off." He smiled. "Just not before the security camera caught the two of them on tape. After they confessed, we sent the boys back to class. Since no one wants to press charges, what's the next step?"

"I'm not even going to go to the DA with this; still there should be some consequences. I have an idea."

She explained what she had in mind, and Brad contacted the family members who'd reported the vandalism and the parents of the perpetrators. Several minutes later, he told Carrie everyone was on board.

"The boys will apologize in person to the victims and commit to doing three hours of chores a month for the next three months, at the convenience of the families. I expect they'll be relieved that the punishment isn't worse, although what their parents decide to do in addition remains to be seen."

"Hopefully, they'll learn from this experience."

"They were frightened when they saw me waiting for them. I don't believe they'll get into any more trouble."

Chapter 26

Ed left the police station and drove to the grocery store to pick up a few items. Back at home, he hung up his coat in the mudroom and walked into the kitchen, Gretchen on his heels, to put the groceries away and brew himself a cup of tea.

Taking the mug into his study, he sat in his leather recliner and stared out toward the water. Contrails of white snaked through the blue sky, a stark contrast to the dark, inky color of the lake and the muddy waves that sluggishly curled onto the beach.

He opened his computer and began writing questions to ask Jill Spencer. She most likely had nothing to do with Alex's murder, but he felt an obligation, at the very least, to rule her out as a suspect.

Several hours later, Annie sauntered into his study.

"You look somber, Ed. Bad day?"

"No. The interviews with Alex's friends went well, and I expect their alibis will check out, although I may want to interview one of them again. We also have another lead." He was about to tell her about Jill Spencer when she interrupted him.

"Martha Kelly mentioned something to me this morning that was a bit of a surprise. Did you know that Alex had been married once before? Her name is Jill Spencer; her maiden name was Clark. It was short-lived, and there were no children. She's an oncology nurse at Newark Hospital; I haven't met her. Her husband, Dan, is a warehouse manager for Mott's. They attend Martha's church."

"Interesting. I was just going to tell you I learned about her from Alex's friends. One of them said the divorce was contentious and Jill was bitter about it. I'm surprised Cheryl didn't say anything to me about her."

"It was a long time ago, Ed. I don't know the woman, but just because Jill Spencer was bitter about losing Alex doesn't mean she would stoop to killing him. I expect Cheryl hasn't thought about her in years and would have no reason to believe she'd be involved in his death. She has other things on her mind right now."

"Any idea why Martha said something to you?"

"She made the remark in passing. We were talking about the murder and all she said was that she wondered how Jill was reacting to the news. People who've lived here all their lives expect the rest of us to know everyone in the community like they do. I had no idea who she was talking about and asked her to explain."

Ed sighed. "I think before I question Jill Spencer, I'll call Cheryl. Perhaps she can provide details about that marriage and why they split. Depending on what she tells me, I'll decide if I want to proceed with the interview or not."

"Slow down, Ed. It's Friday afternoon. How about if you take a break for a couple days and wait until Monday? Remember, we're watching Natasha and Arturo tomorrow afternoon, and we're having dinner with Suzanne and Garrett on Sunday night at their cottage."

"Of course. You're right; it can't hurt for me to put the case aside for a day or two."

"The weather this weekend is supposed to be mild. Suzanne said Garrett is setting up the fire pit; we might be able to have our drinks outside. We're expected at 5:00."

"Anything you want to do before we go over there?"

"Remember, I'm volunteering at the hospital that day."

"That's right. I forgot. What time?"

"I'll be working in the gift shop from nine until noon. There's another volunteer who normally takes that shift;

she asked if I'd switch with her. She'll work my shift from noon to three."

Ed bent down and kissed his wife. "Since we're usually awake by 6:00 because of Gretchen, how about if after walking her we head over to Vic's Diner for an early breakfast before you go to the hospital? They serve Eggs Benedict on Sunday."

"That's a great idea, Ed. I'm looking forward to this weekend."

Chapter 27

Carrie and Matt dropped their children off at 11:00 on Saturday morning and headed to the mall. Ed and Annie played with the children, read to them and then after lunch, Annie put a video on TV for Natasha and carried a dozing Arturo upstairs for a nap. She was just about to enter the bedroom when she pivoted towards Ed, who'd followed behind her. She smiled.

"I'm loving this, Ed. Childhood goes so fast. I remember when our kids and our grandkids were this age. They are so sweet and cuddly. I miss having a baby around."

Ed arched an eyebrow. "Really? You can't be thinking...."

Annie interrupted, laughing. "Ed, duh, of course not. You do remember we're in our 60s? No babies in our future unless there's some sort of miracle or our sons and their wives have more children, and at this point that's highly unlikely."

"Speaking of children," Ed said, "ours will be going to their in-laws for Thanksgiving. Any idea of how you'd like to spend the holiday? It's in two weeks."

"Let me get Arturo settled, and I'll meet you downstairs in a couple minutes." They kept a crib in one of the guest rooms and she was pleased to see the small child nestled down in the cozy, cheery room where their grandchildren, now too old for naps, had slept as infants and toddlers.

A few minutes later, Annie found Ed sitting in the den watching the video with Natasha. He got up and walked into the living room with her where she continued the conversation as though there had been no interruption.

"I completely forgot to tell you that Suzanne has invited us to celebrate the holiday with her, Garrett, and their families at Callaloo, which will be closed to the public for the day."

"That might be fun."

"We met all of them at the wedding, and I'm sure they'd be welcoming, or she wouldn't have invited us; still, I'd feel like a fifth wheel. We'd be the only non-family members there.

"Instead, how would you feel about volunteering at the hospital that day? We could still enjoy Thanksgiving dinner here; I can order a fully cooked meal from the supermarket; we wouldn't have to cook."

"That would work, Annie. If the hospital doesn't need additional volunteers, I have another idea that might please you."

"What's that?"

"We haven't seen Charles for a while. It's short notice; if Michael's not going to be with him and he'd like to visit for a few days, we could pick him up on Tuesday and drive him back to Toronto on Saturday or Sunday."

A professor of Creative Writing at the University of Iowa, Michael was Charles' son and only child, the result of a liaison with a librarian one summer when he was doing research at Cornell.

"I'd love that, Ed. I'll call the volunteer coordinator at the hospital on Monday and see what he says, and if they don't need us, we can call Charles and ask if he'd like to join us."

After the video ended, Annie and Natasha went into the kitchen to make brownies, Arturo, who had awakened from his nap, was keeping them company sitting in the high chair banging spoons. Annie filled a container for the Ramos' and wrapped up the remainder and placed them in the freezer.

Carrie and Matt arrived to collect their children at 4:30 p.m., looking happy and relaxed. Carrie said, "We had a delightful afternoon and thank you both for looking after Natasha and Arturo. We went shopping; I bought a few outfits, one of which I plan to wear when we go back to Brooklyn for Thanksgiving with my family. After we got home, we ordered take-out from The Brewery, Matt put a fire in the fire pit, and we had a picnic, with lots of wine, on our deck overlooking the bay."

She blushed. "We had time to reconnect on another level."

Matt smiled and put his arm around his wife. "Yup, just what the doctor ordered." They all laughed.

Chapter 28

November weather was erratic: some days warm, some cold; some rainy or with snow; and others with sun as bright as a summer day. Sunday evening was mild, with no precipitation forecast. Annie and Ed arrived at Suzanne and Garrett's cottage at 5:00 dressed comfortably in jeans and sweaters, looking forward to spending the early part of the evening enjoying drinks on their patio. They brought two bottles of wine from a Finger Lakes winery to accompany the meal: a spicy Gewurztraminer, and a slightly dry Rosé

The small Victorian cottage, painted indigo blue with white trim, backed up onto a narrow canal that spilled into the bay. White fairy lights were strung through bushes lining the front of the house and on tree trunks in the backyard. They rapped on the brass pineapple-shaped knocker, and within seconds, Garrett opened the lime green door, ushered them inside and enveloped them in hugs.

Inside the cottage, colorful steel drum art and seascapes painted in muted watercolors were hung in groupings throughout the spacious great room. Walls painted vivid blue, lime green and mango set a welcoming backdrop to a sofa and loveseat upholstered in white twill and two new additions: white wicker chairs, cushioned with a vivid floral print with colors picked up from the artwork. Matilda, Suzanne's cat, was draped across one of them, her tail wagging slowly and rhythmically, with one eye open to check out the visitors.

Suzanne was cooking on a five-burner stove in the narrow kitchen. Spices lined a shelf along one wall; with cookbooks set on windowsills and countertops. Exotic aromas wafted through the air. Garrett's law partner, Sheila Caldwell, and her wife, Amy McBride, were sitting on stools at the breakfast bar.

"What a nice surprise!" Annie approached the women and hugged them. "We haven't seen either of you for ages."

"We figured you wouldn't mind our expanding the party," Garrett said. "Sheila and I spend most of our time together discussing legal cases, and Suzanne's parents keep Amy busy. We've been looking forward to an evening away from the pressures of work."

Suzanne glared at her husband then smiled. "It's true," she said in her lilting Jamaican accent. "As much as I hate to admit it, my parents are a bit driven when it comes to the restaurant. Amy works extremely hard."

Amy, a pastry chef, laughed. "But I love it. I wouldn't be doing it if I didn't."

Stepping away from behind the counter, Suzanne, who was wearing skinny black jeans and a teal sweater that set off her dark skin and luminous brown eyes, hugged her friends.

"Welcome. I'm so delighted you're here."

"I smell curry and coconut, Suzanne, and something spicy. My mouth is already watering. What are you cooking?" Annie asked.

"The appetizers, curried coconut chips and fried plantains, are warming in the oven. I'm putting the finishing touches on the jerk chicken."

Tall, broad shouldered, and with dark hair cut short, Garrett, who was of Eastern European Jewish and Puerto Rican ancestry, was wearing jeans and a black turtleneck sweater that flattered his olive skin. His cognac-colored eyes gleamed. "My wife feeds me well. I'm a lucky man!"

Kissing her husband on the check, Suzanne grinned. "In more ways than one, and don't you forget it."

Smiling, Garrett bantered, "And don't you think for one minute that I don't appreciate it."

He continued, "The fire in the fire pit is roaring, and we placed a heater on the patio. I think we can at least have our hors d'oeuvres outside. I made some rum punch, if that's okay with you; if not, we have a fully stocked bar."

A few minutes later, the three couples were sitting comfortably on cushioned wicker chairs, chatting amiably, enjoying drinks and appetizers. The night was clear, with a round, full moon, and a sky thickly carpeted with a profusion of twinkling stars. Suddenly the wind picked up; waves rolled into the bay from the lake, broke along the sea wall and sprayed the group with a fine mist.

Quickly gathering up their drinks and appetizers, they went back inside, sitting on colorful ladder-back chairs at a long, pickled-oak table to partake of the sumptuous meal. In addition to jerk chicken, Suzanne had prepared Jamaican peas and rice, sweet potato salad, and rum cake for dessert.

Ed answered questions about the murder case, but for most of the evening the six friends made light conversation and laughed, a welcome respite.

Before they realized, it was 11:00. "Oh, my, I had no idea it was so late," Annie remarked. "I fear we've completely overstayed our welcome. You all start work earlier than we do, and two of you are driving back to the city," she said, looking at Amy and Sheila, "you're going to be exhausted."

"Annie," Suzanne admonished, "you are one of the best and most dear of my friends. You can never stay too late. My first yoga class isn't until 10:00."

"Our first appointment tomorrow isn't until 9:30," Garrett responded, and Amy said she had the day off; the restaurant was closed on Mondays.

"Can we at least help you clean up?" Ed asked.

Suzanne and Garrett shook their heads. "We have a system, it won't take us long, thanks for offering," Garrett said.

Thanking their hosts and giving and receiving more hugs, Ed and Annie drove home. The weather had changed again. Along with the wind, clouds had rolled in, and a light rain had begun to fall.

Annie sighed. "What a lovely evening. We're really blessed, aren't we, Ed?"

"We are. Good friends, a good meal, and despite the murder, we live in a supportive, safe, and close-knit community. What could be better than that?"

Chapter 29

Ed called Carrie on Monday morning at 9:00 asking if she'd received results of the Spencers' background checks. She said the report had been scanned and emailed to her at 8:00; neither had a criminal record nor firearms registered to them. Ed told Carrie he planned to speak with Cheryl later that morning; after that he'd determine whether to interview the couple or not.

He rang Cheryl Butler's doorbell at 11:15. She answered, looking even more distressed than the last time he saw her.

"Bad day?"

"Each day is a bad day, Ed; today is worse." She explained that she'd received lots of condolence calls and sympathy cards after Alex had been killed. She'd been so busy comforting her children and dealing with her own emotions that she put those aside to read until she felt composed enough to do so.

"I'm touched by all the kind and supportive notes," she started to cry. "For some reason they aren't helping much."

"I hope this is a good time to talk, Cheryl. If not, we can reschedule. When I interviewed Alex's friends, they mentioned he'd been married before, and the divorce was not amicable. What can you tell me about Jill Spencer?"

"You don't need to come back another time; I can talk now. My extended family has departed; the kids will stay for a few more days, but they're out running errands."

She ushered him into the living room, offered him a cup of tea, and a few minutes later they resumed the conversation over steaming cups of Earl Grey.

"There's certainly no love lost between Jill and me, but what happened was a long time ago and I can't imagine her having anything to do with Alex's death. I heard she's happily remarried and that she and her husband recently moved back to Lighthouse Cove. Our paths haven't crossed."

"Whatever you feel comfortable sharing would be appreciated. It will help me decide if I want to interview her and her husband."

Cheryl explained that she, Jill, and Alex had grown up together in Lighthouse Cove.

"Let me go see if I can find our high school yearbook." She left the room and, in a few minutes, came back with the book opened to a page of graduating seniors and pointed. "That's Jill." The young woman was quite beautiful with straight, shoulder-length black hair, large blue eyes, and a small oval face with high cheekbones.

"She was the one all of us envied: captain of the women's tennis team, homecoming queen in our junior and senior years and senior class president. She was comfortable with men, she had a close relationship with her father who took her fishing and hunting, and she bragged about it when they killed a deer. Most of us had trouble killing bugs."

She paused. "Alex was the homecoming king our senior year. He and Jill made a gorgeous couple. I always believed she had her sights set on him; he didn't seem all that interested.

"The three of us ended up going to SUNY Brockport for our undergraduate degrees and remained friends. Jill and Alex started dating winter term during our senior year.

"Jill was a spoiled, willful person who had been indulged by her father. She expected Alex to treat her the same way as he had, and their relationship was contentious. After a few months, Alex confided in me that he was going to break up with her. She must have suspected; Alex had become more and more distant. A few weeks before graduation, she announced she was pregnant.

"Alex could have decided to support the baby after the birth without marrying Jill. But my husband was an honorable man; he didn't want his child to be born out of wedlock and asked Jill to marry him. He vowed to make it work. The wedding was held the day after graduation. I was heartsick about it."

They had been accepted to various colleges in the fall for graduate work: Cheryl to the Bank Street Graduate School of Education in New York City; Jill and Alex to SUNY Buffalo—she for a masters' degree in nursing; Alex for a five-year masters and doctoral program in educational administration. They returned to Lighthouse Cove for summer jobs.

One evening Cheryl and Jill met for dinner at Jill's parents' country club. Jill was drinking heavily. Cheryl admonished her, saying as a nurse she should know better than to drink while she was pregnant. Jill, by now visibly drunk, laughed and confessed she wasn't pregnant. She suspected that Alex was planning to break up with her, and she correctly figured that by faking a pregnancy she could hold on to him.

Jill said in a couple weeks Alex would be with some friends on a fishing trip to the Thousand Islands. During his absence she planned to have a procedure that would assure she couldn't have children because she never wanted them, and say she had a miscarriage with complications that would make her unable to conceive in the future. If he suggested adopting, she'd tell him it would be too emotionally painful when she couldn't have her own.

She knew he'd be upset that she hadn't called him, but she'd respond that it had happened quickly and at the time he was on a boat on the St. Lawrence River, and she'd been unable to reach him.

"She was certain he'd believe her and that would be the end of it; they could get on with their lives the way she'd planned all along. I was about to ask her how she was able to avoid becoming pregnant since she hadn't yet had the procedure, when it was almost as if she read my mind. She'd been careful, she confided, and nothing ever happened to her that she didn't want to happen. She said she always got her way."

Cheryl didn't know what to do. She and Alex had been friends since childhood, and she loathed deception and was appalled by what Jill had done, but before she could decide, the situation was taken out of her hands.

Alarmed that she'd been so indiscreet, Jill called Cheryl the next morning. Alex had gone to the grocery store, and she said she didn't have much time and implored Cheryl to keep their conversation a secret. As she was talking, Alex entered the apartment; he'd taken his car keys but forgotten his wallet.

He overheard the entire conversation, and when it ended, he confronted her. At first, she denied he'd heard correctly, then she verbally attacked him for eavesdropping.

"Alex guessed she'd been talking with me and said that if he called me, he knew I would tell him the truth."

Cornered, Jill admitted to him that she'd faked the pregnancy, but begged forgiveness and promised never to lie to him again. He didn't believe her; they separated and within months the marriage was dissolved. That fall, Jill matriculated as planned to Buffalo for her graduate work, Alex transferred to Syracuse University, and Cheryl began classes at Bank Street. She and Alex stayed in contact, and the following summer started dating. They married two years later.

"Did you hear from Jill again?"

"No. Though for a while after she and Alex split, she called him several times and when he didn't answer his phone, she left messages for him to call her back. When he didn't respond, she started emailing him. In one of those emails, she wrote that she hoped someday he would understand how it felt to lose someone.

"She was emotionally distraught when she made that statement. I don't believe she meant it and if she still had feelings for him, I'd be the one she'd go after, not him. It was a misguided and desperate attempt to reconcile with him. He erased the phone messages and blocked her on his computer, and that ended it. He never heard from her again.

"My husband was a good man, Ed. He treated me and our children kindly, and we all adored him. He didn't deserve to be killed, but I can't imagine Jill being the one who ended his life."

On his way home, Ed stopped to see Carrie and summarized his conversation with Cheryl Butler.

"Are you still going to interview Jill Spencer?" Carrie asked

"Yes. Cheryl doesn't believe Jill killed Alex; still, I'd like to rule her out as a suspect. Then, there's her husband. We know nothing about him or what Jill told him that might have set him off."

"I think I should send Brad with you when you interview them."

"I agree."

"Ed, when I did the background check, I discovered they don't have a landline."

"We do live in challenging times," Ed grinned.

"So, how will you contact them? Getting their cell phone numbers might take some time."

"Easy. I'll see if I can locate each of them at work."

He held up his right index finger. "Give me a minute," he said and doing a search on his cell phone, found and dialed the hospital number. He spoke with several people until he got the answer he needed. Jill Spencer was not working that day. Then he called Mott's. Dan was expected between 3:30 and 4:00.

"That does it," he explained to Carrie. "I'll grab Brad and head over to their house, if we're lucky they'll both be there."

"If they're not?"

"We have lots of options. For starters, I'll tack a sealed note on their front door with my business card asking that they call me. If they have nothing to hide, they'll contact me quickly out of curiosity."

"If they don't?"

"Hopefully it won't come to that, but I suppose the next step would be to get a search warrant so we can get into the house to check and see if they have shotguns or other suspicious evidence lying about."

"That shouldn't be a problem. Good luck."

Chapter 30

Several minutes later, the two investigators arrived at the Spencer house, a tidy, butter-colored Cape Cod with white trim, cornflower blue shutters and a cluster of rhododendron and azalea bushes on either side of a matching blue front door. As they pulled into a parking space in front of the house, a tall, heavy-set brown-haired man with guileless hazel eyes and an open face unlatched the door and started walking toward them. He was wearing a plaid flannel shirt, blue jeans, and brown oxford shoes.

"Can I help you?" he asked pleasantly.

The two men pulled out their ID cards and introduced themselves.

"I'm Dan Spencer. Why are you here?"

Ed replied that he and Detective Washington were investigating the murder of Alex Butler and were reaching out to those with information that might help them solve the case.

Dan sighed. "I heard about the mayor's death. I'm sorry he's dead, but I don't believe there's anything my wife or I could tell you that would help solve his murder. You're probably here because you know he and Jill were once married, but their marriage ended a long time ago, and she's not had any contact with him since they split."

"That's why we want to speak with her, but we'd also like to talk with you," Ed responded.

"I was on my way to work, Jill will be home shortly, she has the day off and is out running errands." He looked at his watch. "I need to call my boss to let him know I'll be late."

"We'll try to keep this brief."

Once inside the house, Dan guided them to the living room and pointed to two yellow and cornflower-blue floral-printed upholstered chairs that sat across from a blue sofa with yellow and white accent pillows that faced a fireplace. A variety of photos had been placed on the white mantel; Ed assumed, since there were none of children, that the couple was childless.

"Sit there." He pointed to the chairs. "I'll sit across from you on the sofa with Jill when she gets back."

While they waited, the three men made small talk, Dan glancing at his watch every minute or so.

After several minutes, he said, "I don't know what's keeping her, she should have been home by now. I expect you also know that she faked a pregnancy to get Alex Butler to marry her, and that the divorce was contentious. When I was offered the job at Mott's she was reluctant to move back to Lighthouse Cove and pleaded with me to not take it. It made no sense because her parents were here, and she was close to her father.

"I asked her why she was so opposed to relocating, and she told me about what she'd done. It was a secret she'd held onto for so long that it was eating her up inside and when we started dating, she didn't know how to tell me. It had nothing to do with us, and she's not the same woman as she was back them. I assured her that our relationship was strong.

"If she'd said something about it when we started dating it wouldn't have mattered, but she had no way of knowing that. People make mistakes. It was a horrible thing to do, and she regrets it, especially now since he's dead and she never apologized to him. She contemplated getting in touch with Cheryl, then decided that it's probably for the best to let sleeping dogs lie."

They heard the rumbling of a car engine, then it stopped. Dan strolled over to one of the two double hung windows that flanked the front door. Ed and Brad followed.

"She's here," Dan said as they watched a tall, slender, dark-haired woman get out of a blue Ford Bronco that she'd parked in the driveway.

Her hair was pulled back into a ponytail, and she was wearing slim jeans, low cut brown leather boots, and a stylish brown leather jacket over what appeared to be an ivory silk shirt. She opened the trunk and pulled out a couple sacks of groceries. When she entered the living room and noticed Ed and Brad, she hesitated.

"Dan, who are these men, and why are you still here? I thought you'd be on your way to work by now."

"Hi, honey." Her husband took the groceries from her and introduced them. "They're from the police department; they know about your history with Alex Butler and want to speak with us about his murder." He sniffed the air.

"Do I smell cigarette smoke?"

Jill sighed. "I went to Apex and filled the car with gas. The machine at the pump didn't print out my receipt, and I had to go into the store to get it. Several men were standing outside smoking." She grimaced. "When we're finished here, I'm going to take a shower, my hair must stink."

She glanced at Ed. "I overheard the men talking about Alex. I didn't recognize them, and they seemed a bit scruffy. I wonder if they had something to do with his death."

"Or they could have just been discussing his murder; it is pretty big news around here," he responded.

"Of course, that's probably it. I'm sorry Alex was killed. What happened between us was a long time ago, and he was a good man. We've had no contact since our divorce; that was a long time ago. Who told you about us?"

Ed shook his head. "It doesn't matter."

"It probably wasn't Cheryl; she'd know I'm not capable of killing anyone; it must have been Alex's friends. They've been tight as thieves since middle school. They don't like me. I'm not surprised after what I did to him."

Dan took the groceries into the kitchen and returned with a glass of water for his wife and sat down next to her.

Ed said, "I might as well get to the point. A Remington 12-gauge shotgun killed Alex. We checked, and there aren't any guns registered to either of you, but there are other ways to obtain them. Would either of you be in possession of one?'

Dan shook his head, "I don't care for guns and never have hunted."

"I used to hunt with my father," Jill admitted. "I did it mainly so I could spend time with him. He died last year, since then I've had no desire to shoot a gun."

"Neither of us killed him," Dan said. "We'd have no reason to want him dead."

Ed responded, "Please bear with me. The questions are routine. To rule you out, would you give us permission to search your property?"

Dan looked at Jill. "We have nothing to hide. Honey, you okay with this?"

Jill shrugged. "Sure."

Brad left the room to conduct the search. Jill touched her husband's arm and looked at Ed. "My husband needs to get to work. How much longer do you think this will take?"

"Not much longer."

"I understand why you're here, but what happened was a long time ago. I was a willful and spoiled child when I manipulated Alex into marrying me. As I matured, I realized what a stupid thing I'd done. As you can see, I've moved on." She took her husband's hand in hers and smiled at him.

Just then Brad entered the room, shaking his head. "No guns. I searched the house, their garage and inside their cars."

"One more thing: Do you remember what you were doing last Tuesday morning?"

"I was working two shifts back-to-back that day," Jill volunteered. "Before you leave, I'll give you my supervisor's contact information."

Ed looked at her husband. "And you?"

"I was visiting another warehouse owned by our parent company." A desk was sitting in a corner of the room; he walked over to it, opened a drawer, pulled out a business card and gave it to Ed. "Here's the contact information for the manager there. She can verify I was with her all day."

Ed thanked the couple for speaking with them. "We can let ourselves out."

While Brad drove to the station, Ed texted Carrie to let her know they were on their way back and that while he thought she should check the Spencer's alibis, he felt certain that the couple had nothing to do with Alex's murder.

Minutes later, sitting with Brad in her office, he said, "We probably should check out the men Jill spotted at Apex, too. The forensic techs found cigarette butts at the site, none of the DNA on them matched any in the database. There must be cameras; we could probably look at the video and see if facial recognition software can identify any of the men."

Ed handed Carrie the card Dan Spencer had given him and a piece of paper with Jill's supervisor's name and contact information.

"Let's wait until we confirm theirs; after that I'll call the store manager," Carrie said. "I don't believe Alex's murderers would be talking about his death in front of Apex, but until we know for sure, we can't rule them out."

Ed and Brad waited while Carrie placed the calls to Jill's supervisor and the manager of the plant Dan had visited. Their alibis were quickly confirmed.

Carrie then called the Apex manager. He said he'd be happy to give her the tapes, but he knew the men. They were hunters from Virginia who rented a cottage in Lighthouse Cove each year for several days in November. Decent guys who had arrived earlier that morning after driving through the night, which could explain why Jill had thought they looked scruffy; they hadn't had time to shower or shave.

They had filled their car with gas, gone into the store to purchase coffee, and then waited outside for the owner of the cottage to arrive to give them the keys to the cottage. He hadn't seen any of them smoking, but he was busy with customers and admitted he wasn't paying attention. They must have heard about the mayor's death and were discussing it when Jill showed up.

Audio #3—Betsey Cooper

Fair-skinned with green eyes like her brother, Betsey was sold when she was eight to a plantation in South Carolina and assigned to work as a seamstress in the master's house. For reasons unknown, at age 13 she was exiled to the plantation's rice fields where she toiled from dawn to dusk building dykes and levees and stripping kernels of rice from their spiky stalks.

Aided by a group of Quakers with a passion for justice, the young woman escaped with others through the Underground Railroad during a lunar eclipse in March 1859. After perilous travel fraught with danger, she arrived at Macyville in June of the same year, where she was reunited with her brother.

A few months after her arrival, settlers at Macyville learned that slave trackers from the south had discovered the location of the fugitives. Within hours, they ushered the frightened group onto a schooner owned by ship captain Samuel Weatherfield who transported them across Lake Ontario to safety in Thomastown, Canada. It was believed, but never proven, that a Lighthouse Cove businessman, harboring resentment towards Benjamin Macy, had alerted the trackers.

Betsey arrived in Thomastown in December and was welcomed into the home of Henry and Anna Fitzhugh, an abolitionist couple who doted on her and treated her like the daughter they'd never had. Within weeks, the young woman obtained employment as a seamstress at a dry goods store owned by a free man of color named Josiah Cooper, and his son, William, and shortly after moved into her own cottage.

Uneducated but intelligent, Betsey was eager to learn. In the evenings, after the store closed, William tutored her; within a short time, she and Abraham began to correspond. Her brother and his family traveled across Lake Ontario to attend Betsey's wedding to William a year later, and again for the christenings of their children: Nathaniel, born in 1863; Serena, born a year later.

The Civil War ended; the Coopers remained in Canada. Betsey died of ill health in 1889, the result of the abuse and mistreatment she'd experienced while working in the rice fields. William died in 1902. Generations later, many of their descendants immigrated back to the States, settling in the Finger Lakes region of New York.

Chapter 31

Unlike murder cases on TV, most aren't quite as simple to solve as people believe. The forensic techs had not been able to link the evidence they collected at the crime scene with any DNA on file, and the investigators were striking out with viable leads. Ed decided to take a break to attend the monthly lunch with his Navy buddies (they called themselves the ROMEOs, Retired Old Men Eating Out).

They met at Phillips House, a restaurant that stood high on a hill overlooking acres of apple orchards, and in the distance, a view of the lake. It was a blustery, grey day and Ed was struck by how the apple trees—weeks earlier fertile with heavy, ripened fruit—were now barren, their twisted, gnarled limbs dark silhouettes against the brown landscape.

The men congregated at a table near the fireplace where fragrant applewood logs burned brightly. Each ordered the special: a cup of homemade chicken noodle soup, a turkey club sandwich, and coffee. Beverages arrived first, and the men held up their mugs to toast their friendship.

Larry Mandel, a widower who had recently remarried a woman he'd met at a class at the community college, reported that he and Francie had purchased a home in Ft. Myers, Florida, and would be spending their winters there. The cold weather had made his arthritis worse.

Jeff Ketchum had recently married his long-time girlfriend, a financial planner. They would spend the winter sailing the turquoise waters of the Caribbean on his sailboat.

Like Ed and Annie, Bob Fergus and his wife usually spent their winters in Lighthouse Cove. This year they had rented a cottage overlooking the Pacific Ocean in Laguna Beach, California, for February, to visit with their son and his family who lived nearby in Laguna Niguel.

Ed filled them in on the murder case and lack of suspects. His friends offered support and encouragement, reminding him that he always solved his cases—sometimes it just took a bit longer than he expected.

Larry, sensing that Ed might want a break from discussing the investigation, changed the subject and asked if anyone had heard of an organization called Citizens for Progress. None of them had.

"Why?" Bob said.

"I was at the supermarket yesterday and when I came out, there were fliers on all the cars in the parking lot with information about it. When I got home, I went onto their website and learned that it was started by two brothers—Robert and Steven Swain. The members are a small group of citizens who think that our zoning laws are too restrictive and that there are too many properties that aren't on the tax rolls because of their non-profit status.

"They're trying to get candidates to run for public office who will favor changing the laws to allow for more commercial, residential, and industrial development. For that to happen, they'll have to win during the primaries next April and against their competitors in the general election next fall."

"Anybody know anything about the Swains?" asked Ed. "Their names aren't familiar to me."

"I called a couple people I thought might know something about them. What I learned is that both men live in the community—Steven in a new townhouse development across from the marinas, shops, and restaurants along Rt.14, and Robert in a farmhouse on several acres of land just outside the village. Until they organized CFP, they appeared to keep pretty much to themselves."

"I can only imagine what Annie will say when she hears about this," Ed remarked.

"For years The Nature Conservancy owned the land where Macyville is being reconstructed; they deeded it to the historical society after they received the grant to restore it. She's had plenty of offers to sell all or part of it to developers. Of course, she wouldn't nor can she because of a legal agreement with the Conservancy in cooperation with the National Trust. I wonder if that project was the tipping point for these people. The land is worth millions and is prime real estate."

The men thought that elected officials were doing just fine keeping a balance between preservation and development, and agreed that they didn't think the group would be terribly successful. They spent the next hour in companionable conversation.

Realizing that his closest friends would soon be scattering and that the monthly lunches would cease until spring, Ed gave another toast to wish them safe travels. He would miss spending time with them. Their friend George's death had created a void in their group, and he realized not only how fleeting life can be but that it could change in an instant. He prayed silently that they would all survive the winter and remain healthy.

Chapter 32

Annie arrived at work the next morning and found a stack of mail on her desk. Jason's car was in the parking lot—he must have collected it before going upstairs. The return address on one piece was from the National Trust for Historic Preservation.

Several months earlier, she and Alex had written and applied for a second grant, this time to hire a writer who would create a book about Freedom Hill and the history of Macyville, as a companion to the exhibit.

The competition was stiff, she knew; she expected either a rejection letter or notification of receiving only part of the money, especially since the historical society had received the grant from the same organization for the reconstruction of Macyville. She took a deep breath and opened the letter.

"We are happy to inform you......" Annie continued to read and pumped a fist. "Yes!" She called Jason on the intercom.

"Jason, we got the grant! The entire amount. We'll be able to do an RFP to hire someone to write the book. Hopefully, we can have it ready for the grand opening on July 4 and sell it in the gift shop there."

"That's fabulous, Annie. Congratulations!"

"You played a part in this, too, Jason, by helping to write sections of the grant. Let's plan to have a nice, long lunch to celebrate sometime after the holidays—my treat."

"I'd love that, Annie."

She changed the subject. "In the meantime, I should probably email the board members and let them know about it. While I'm doing that would you please write a press release and send it to the local news outlets?"

"I'll get on that right now and have it completed before we break for lunch."

Annie was so excited, she started to call Ed then remembered he was interviewing Chris Bayley again.

Logging into her computer, she started emailing the board members when the museum phone rang. She answered, and after ending the conversation, grimaced and rolled her eyes.

Chapter 33

The investigators were sitting around the table in the interview view room when Chris Bayley arrived at 8:30, armed with a box of warm apple crullers, a bottle of fresh apple cider, and paper cups.

"Peace offering," he said. "The farm stand near my house is still open, and I thought you'd enjoy these—the crullers are the best I've ever tasted. I apologize, I can't stay. I have a meeting to get to."

Carrie looked at the man, not believing what she was hearing. The two others shook their heads in bewilderment.

"I suspect you thought I was withholding information when you interviewed me and my friends after Alex was killed. I was, but it didn't have anything to do with his murder. What I reported was true. He simply didn't want to ask me about an internship for his son during the poker game—and for the record— I did learn we hire summer interns.

"I admit to being distracted that morning; that's probably what you picked up on. I'm working on a case that's taking up a lot of my time. I can't disclose the details, but I can tell you it's a big one. If you'd been a bit more forthcoming when you asked me to come here for another interview, I would have told you that, and we could have avoided this meeting.

"I want Alex's murderer to be caught as much as you do. Have you contacted Jill Spencer yet?"

"We have. She and her husband are in the clear."

"Then if there's nothing more, I really do need to leave." He turned around and walked out the door. "See you around."

The investigators grinned at each other, embarrassed that they hadn't considered arranging to speak with Chris over the phone, then munched on the crullers and drank the cider, admitting they were delicious.

Having nothing more to discuss for the moment, Carrie and Brad went back to their offices while Ed stayed in the interview room to finish writing his report about the interviews with Alex's friends. As he was finishing up, Carrie reentered the room.

"Sometimes I hate this job."

"Why?"

"I just had a phone call from a man who wanted to lodge a complaint against Annie."

"Annie? Whatever for?"

"His name is Robert Swain and he's formed a group with his brother, Steven, called Citizens for Progress. They requested a booth at the museum's Holiday Festival of Lights to try and generate interest in their mission. She declined his request because she didn't want to politicize the event."

"I just heard about them, Carrie. When I had lunch with my friends yesterday, one of them mentioned that CFP had placed fliers on car windshields in the supermarket parking lot. They want the community to elect new municipal officials who favor changing our zoning laws."

"Until a few minutes ago, I'd never heard of them either. I called Janice, figuring as mayor she probably would know something about them, and she did. She said she thinks this whole initiative started after the zoning board turned down requests for variances that the Swain brothers requested for two projects.

"They own a family cottage on the corner of Wickham Blvd. and 3rd Street that's been vacant for years. They tried selling it last summer but were asking too much—it's apparently in terrible condition. When they couldn't sell it, they decided they wanted to tear it down and build a carwash."

"A carwash?" Ed laughed.

"Yes. Their rationale was that the closest one is ten miles away, so they'd be providing a service for the community. It's not happening. The zoning board wouldn't grant a variance for a commercial endeavor in a residential neighborhood.

"Janice said they also wanted to buy the vacant church located on the corner of Bay and Lake streets to build a boaters' bar. There are docks behind the property, but again, the zoning isn't appropriate; it's zoned single family residential/non-profit, and the church refused to sell it to them. As you know, a group of artists and history buffs purchased it to open a maritime art gallery and antique boat museum."

"Why did Robert call you?"

"He believed I could overrule Annie's decision and tell her it was against the law to exclude his group; he said they have a right to assemble. I couldn't do that and when he insisted that I speak with her, I refused. As if that would work." She laughed.

"I reminded him that the historical society land is privately owned, she could legally prohibit anyone from attending.

"He made a bunch of noise about showing up anyway. I advised him that while he certainly was welcome to attend the festivities, if he arrived with a table and promotional materials, I'd arrest him for trespassing.

"He was terribly displeased and threatened to go to my superiors. I said I'd have no problem with him doing that, I can't imagine he'd get any support from them. Our mayor and board of trustees are among those his group is targeting to replace."

Ed shook his head. "I can only imagine how angry Annie was about the request."

Carrie smiled. "I'm sure you'll find out this evening. Anyway, as much as I had hoped Matt, the kids, and I could attend the festival as a family, it appears Mia and I might have to work that evening to make sure the Swains and their minions don't show up to disrupt the festivities."

"I'm just about finished here. I think I'll go over to the lighthouse and talk with Annie."

Annie wasn't as upset as he'd predicted—just annoyed. She expected that the brothers would have little success in their mission and by the time spring rolled around, they'd be disbanded.

Chapter 34

As it turned out, the hospital had more than enough volunteers for Thanksgiving Day. Several high school seniors, as part of their graduation requirement to take on a community service project, were serving the meals for staff and visitors, and members of a Jehovah's Witness congregation were working at the gift shop.

Ed called Charles. Michael would be at his mother's and adopted father's in Detroit for Thanksgiving. Instead of celebrating the holiday in Lighthouse Cove, the retired professor suggested they spend it with him in Toronto. That way they wouldn't have to make two round trips to pick him up and bring him back, and they could see his new home.

He'd moved recently from a condo on the outskirts of the city to a townhouse in Yorkville and said that he had plenty of room for Gretchen if they wanted to bring her along. Annie was delighted—the couple's passports were up to date, as were Gretchen's vaccination records.

The Wednesday before Thanksgiving, Ed secured the pet hammock in the back of the SUV with Gretchen's favorite stuffed bunny and a soft blanket so she could travel comfortably, placed her on the car seat, and tethered her lead to a seat belt.

They weren't expected until after lunch and decided to drive the scenic route, along the Lake Ontario Parkway. The two-lane road meandered for miles along the lake, skirting wetlands, wheat-colored sea grasses, desolate, stark beaches, and picnicking sites. A few fluffy, white clouds danced their way across the bright blue sky. They observed a muskrat slithering from a muddy bank into the water and a flock of honking geese flying high overhead as they journeyed south for the winter.

At the end of the parkway, the Lewiston-Queenston Bridge spanned the Niagara River and on the other side intersected with the Queen Elizabeth Way, or QEW, a major Canadian highway that started near Buffalo and ended in Toronto, the fourth largest city in North America.

Before reaching the bridge, the couple took a short detour to Olcott Beach, a charming western New York hamlet, where they could walk Gretchen and eat lunch. Assuming that most restaurants there would be closed this time of year, Annie had packed a picnic lunch: Provencal tuna sandwiches, veggie chips and the brownies she and Natasha had baked the Saturday they'd babysat her and Arturo.

An old-fashioned working carousel was the focal point of the lakeside park that during summer months attracted residents and tourists to Sunday afternoon concerts performed under a gazebo built in the 1890s. They strolled the length of a wooden boardwalk, Gretchen sniffing at picnic tables that had been secured against the doors and windows of an eclectic mix of shops and restaurants, now closed for the season.

The day was cold, in the low 30s. Ed parked in a spot overlooking the lake where they sat in the heated car and ate their lunch, talking quietly. Gretchen, tired from their walk, was fast asleep on the backseat.

At 3:00, Ed parked the car in front of a large, Federal-style brick townhouse; Charles greeted them at the front door with hugs.

"Charles, you look wonderful!" Annie handed him a gift bag with a couple of bottles of his favorite Bordeaux, a homemade loaf of whole wheat orange quick bread, and some jams she'd purchased at farmstands the previous summer.

"I'm so pleased with the gifts," Charles said. "Thank you. It's completely unnecessary but much appreciated."

"I know you like sweet breads for breakfast, Charles, and thought you'd enjoy a taste of Lighthouse Cove with the jams. I also seem to remember that this Bordeaux is one of your favorites."

Annie peered closely at him. "There's something different about you. Oh my, you're wearing jeans. And a turtleneck. And sneakers. I don't think I've ever seen you wearing anything other than perfectly pressed slacks, a tailored shirt and a sport coat with polished dress shoes or on more casual days, a sweater over your shirt with a bowtie."

The 77-year-old blushed. "It's my son's influence. He says that the 70s are the new 50s, and the way I've been dressing makes me look like an old man. He's even encouraged me to register at one of those online senior dating sites."

He laughed. "Annie, I'm way past that. I am an old man, although the medications I've been taking for my heart condition and Parkinsons' disease certainly are helping me feel better and younger. I must admit I'm getting used to these, they're extremely comfortable." He smoothed down his jeans.

"They flatter you," Ed chimed in, looking with amusement at the small, white-haired man.

Charles blushed again, ushered them into the house and immediately led them upstairs to a beautifully appointed guestroom with a circa 1850s working gas fireplace. Annie unpacked their clothing and Ed took Gretchen out for a short walk. When he returned, his wife and Charles were sitting in the parlor on wing chairs by a roaring fire, drinking glasses of the rich, red Bordeaux wine he'd decanted from one of the bottles the DeCleryks had brought.

"Come in and take a seat," Charles said to Ed, handing him a glass of wine. "Annie was telling me about Alex Butler's death. He was still superintendent of schools when I lived in Lighthouse Cove, so I really didn't know him. I do remember he was well-regarded. What a tragedy."

Annie's eyes welled up. "Ed and I started socializing with him and his wife after he became a member of my board of directors. You would have liked him; he was bright and gentle. His death is a real loss to our community."

Charles looked at Ed. "I'm assuming you're working on the case. Any suspects?"

"I am, with Brad Washington—he's a detective who joined the police department after Carrie was appointed chief. This is a tough one. We've had leads, nothing has panned out."

"I hope something breaks so you can solve the case soon."

Ed nodded somberly. Annie, believing it was time to change the subject, said, "I'm curious about why you decided to sell your condo, Charles. Your new home is beautiful, but it must be a lot more work to maintain."

"I was bored, Annie, and it was hard to meet people. Now I have neighbors who are happy to socialize, and the younger ones shovel my walk when it snows and rake the leaves from my yard in the fall. I park the car in a municipal garage around the corner, so I don't have to worry about scraping snow and ice from it when we have a snowstorm. There's a garden in the back where I can putter, and a library.

"My library can be converted into a bedroom if I ever need to live on one floor, and I've installed a full bath where the powder room used to be. This is just a better fit for me, plus I can walk to shops and restaurants. Before we go to dinner, I'll take you on a tour."

"Still, it's a large home for one person to roam around in, Charles," Ed noted.

"Michael doesn't have tenure at Iowa yet. He's considering applying for a job here in Toronto—there are several colleges with excellent creative writing departments. Should he desire, he can live with me until he gets settled. I'm hoping he'll marry and have a family someday. After I'm gone, he'll inherit this house."

"I hope it's not too soon," Annie remarked. Her antipathy to Charles' son was related to his peripheral involvement in the death of her friend, Emily Bradford; still she was pleased that he had developed a close relationship with his father.

They finished their wine and made sure that Gretchen was settled with a chewy bone to keep her occupied; then Annie, Ed and Charles walked two blocks for an early dinner at a Thai restaurant where they feasted on a variety of fragrant and spicy specialties. A couple hours later, sated from the food, they strolled back to Charles' house and, exhausted, were asleep by 10 p.m.

Chapter 35

The next morning, Ed and Annie awoke to the smell of fragrant, rich coffee and baking bread. Making their way to the kitchen, they were greeted by their friend, who turned around just as he was pulling sweet rolls from the oven. Gretchen stared intently at Charles, hoping for a handout.

"She must have pried your bedroom door open. She's been with me for at least half an hour. I took her out and then fed her." He bent down to pet her.

"Thanks for looking after her," Annie replied.

"Did you sleep well?"

"We slept like logs," Ed replied. "The bed is extremely comfortable. We hope you don't mind, but we kept a small fire going. It was cozy and comforting. Gretchen slept in front of it all night."

"Not a problem. It's why I converted all the fireplaces to gas after I moved in—much cleaner and easier to maintain."

Gretchen pawed Charles' leg. "It appears she's still starving from the look on her face." He slipped her a small piece of warm roll.

Annie replied, "As little as she is, she's a chow hound and, according to her, she never has enough food. I'll give her a mint-flavored dental bone in a few minutes. By the way, the rolls smell wonderful."

"I can't take credit for these," Charles admitted. "They're from the grocery story, and all I had to do was bake them. The coffee, however, is my doing. I purchase fresh-roasted beans from a local purveyor and grind them myself.

"Annie, I remember you typically take tea in the morning. I have PG Tips and milk and honey if you'd like that instead of the coffee."

"That's very considerate, Charles, but that coffee smells so delicious that I think this morning I'll have a cup of it instead. I expect I'll want a cup of the tea later in the day."

He handed each of his friends a mug and pointed to the countertop. "Cream, sugar, and even a little bit of Bailey's Irish Cream, if you'd like a little tot of something to wake you up. Please, don't stand on ceremony. Help yourselves."

Placing the plate of rolls on the kitchen table, along with a bowl of fresh fruit, he said, "I can make you something hardier, if you'd prefer."

"We ate so much last night, Charles, I'm not hungry," Annie responded. "This is perfect. Plus, we have a feast to look forward to this evening."

For the Thanksgiving meal, Charles had ordered a full complement of ingredients from a local grocery store. A small turkey, fresh cranberries, oranges, celery, brussels sprouts, mushrooms, and salad greens filled the refrigerator. Sweet potatoes, a small container of maple syrup, pecans, onions, canned chicken broth, shelled, vacuum-packed chestnuts, a loaf of crusty bread and two bakery pies, one pumpkin and the other, pecan, had been tucked away in the pantry.

They spent the day cooking, and by late afternoon the house was redolent with the smell of roasting turkey and all the fixings. At 4:30, after feeding and walking Gretchen, they sat in the living room and toasted their friendship with a glass of spicy Zinfandel for Annie and small tumblers of single malt scotch for Charles and Ed. They sat down at 5:30 to a sumptuous feast at the mahogany dining room table, set with shimmering candles, fine linens, crystal goblets, lustrous silverware, and heirloom dishes.

Chapter 36

Friday morning dawned clear and bright. Charles had arranged for a neighbor's daughter, home for the weekend from college, to look after Gretchen for the day, and after breakfast, Ed, Annie and Charles drove to the Royal Ontario Museum to view the permanent Dale Chihuly glass exhibit. After a quick lunch in the museum's café, they visited the Botanical Garden, festively decorated for the season.

By now, it was midafternoon, and they stopped at a charming tearoom for tea and pastries. Charles said that before heading home he wanted to make another stop—it was a surprise for them. Soon after, they approached a neighborhood that was crowded with modern skyscrapers, high rise condos and trendy shops. After pulling into a parking garage, Charles led them around the corner to an alley where a three-story red-brick Victorian stood between a clothing boutique and a gift shop.

A black metal sign embossed with gold lettering stated that the Museum of History and Archeology was owned and maintained by the University of Toronto. Charles punched a code into a keypad and ushered his friends inside.

"I wanted you to see this. For now, it's only open for private, pre-arranged tours, but we're hoping by spring to open it to the public."

Annie glanced around at the open exhibit space. "How charming."

Charles responded, "I'm the president of the board of trustees for the museum. It's another reason why I wanted to move back into the city. This is within walking distance to my house.

"Ed, do you remember when you visited the university when you were investigating Emily

Bradford's murder that the dean showed you a room with Thomas Battleforth's manuscript and other artifacts from an archaeological dig?"

"I do."

"Well, we moved all those items over here along with artifacts and memorabilia that were discovered at other digs. We were simply running out of space. There are two more floors with exhibits above this one."

Intrigued, the couple wandered through the building. In addition to a scale model of the village where Battleforth had lived and a copy of his manuscript, there were also artifacts from the War of 1812, including copies of letters that had been written by Lighthouse Cove resident Rebecca Fitzhugh to her sister during a journey to England to find her husband, Robert, whom she believed had been taken prisoner of war.

Thomastown, where Fitzhugh's abolitionist son Henry had settled after his father died, was the focus of another exhibit, with artifacts and written materials that tied that community to Lighthouse Cove before and during the Civil War.

Annie wandered through the space, admiring jewelry, cookware, copies of letters in glass cases, and on one wall, a framed newspaper article with a photo of a handsome dark-skinned man standing next to a comely fair-skinned woman with light eyes who was seated next to him on a wooden chair.

Below, a headline announced that the Coopers had purchased another dry goods store. The article indicated that the store would be the third for the family and where William Cooper's wife, Betsey, would be designing custom-made dresses for the women of the village. The article gave information about Betsey's history and how she had learned to sew while enslaved at the Swain Plantation in Charleston, South Carolina.

Excited, Annie called Ed over to the exhibit.

"Read this, Ed. We know Betsey and her brother were separated as children, and she was sold to a plantation in South Carolina, but if Alex knew the name of it or that it was in Charleston, he didn't include that in his audio descriptions, perhaps for the sake of brevity.

"It's the same name as the men who are involved in that group, CFP. That's not a terribly common name. Look at that photo. Betsey was beautiful. She started out working as a house slave which is where she learned to sew but for some reason was sent to work in the rice fields."

"Where are you going with this, Annie?"

"You know what happened to comely female slaves, Ed. It's entirely possible that as she grew older, she attracted the attention of the master. Let's assume she got pregnant with his child. She was half white, the baby would most likely be light skinned, too. In some slave owning families, it wasn't uncommon for those babies to be taken from their mothers to live with the master's family. Maybe that's why she was sent to work in the rice fields. They wouldn't have wanted her to have contact with the child.

"We have no information that she gave birth to a child while in captivity, but if she did, it might have been so traumatic for her that after she escaped, she never talked about it."

Ed shook his head. "I'm still not understanding where you're going with this, Annie."

Frustrated, Annie replied, "I know I'm speculating, but could it be possible that the baby grew up unaware of its Black heritage, and after many years a branch of the family ended up in our part of New York? Maybe Alex discovered that the Swains are his relatives and after he contacted them, they killed him to keep it secret."

"Annie, I think it's a stretch," Ed admonished. "I don't agree with the mission of CFP; the brothers are greedy, which is why they formed it, but to believe they killed Alex? Really?

"I think you want them to be guilty of something because you're angry about CFP and their complaint to Carrie because you wouldn't give them a booth at the Festival of Lights."

"That's preposterous. Ed, you should know me better than that. I am not a vindictive person. I freely admit they're not at the top of my favorite people list, but that doesn't mean I want them to be charged for a crime they didn't commit. What I want is for you to find Alex's killer, and I'm trying to help you by thinking out of the box."

Ed turned to Charles, who, bemused, had merely observed. "I apologize. You brought us here to show us this museum, and now we're arguing about who might have killed Alex Butler."

Charles grinned. "You two are the happiest and most well-adjusted couple I've ever met. When I lived in Lighthouse Cove, I never saw you argue. It's kind of refreshing to learn that even you have squabbles."

He laughed. "I'm enjoying this; it's fascinating. Please continue."

"Annie," Ed said, "there must be hundreds of people with the name Swain. If their last name was Jones, would you want us to question every person who lived near Lighthouse Cove with the name Jones to see if they murdered Alex?"

"Of course not, but you know this is different."

Ed threw his hands up, conceding. "I'll call Carrie on Monday and see what she wants to do."

They spent the next hour viewing the rest of the exhibits; then Charles drove to his home. Originally, they had planned on dining at an intimate French bistro but tired and wanting to spend time with Gretchen, who it appeared had thoroughly enjoyed her day with the neighbor's daughter, they instead ate leftovers from the night before.

Chapter 37

The next morning, Charles had another surprise for Ed and Annie. A few years earlier, Ed had discovered a rusted metal box on the beach in Lighthouse Cove containing valuables belonging to England's royal family that had been believed to have been lost at sea in the 1700s. The items were returned to the monarchy and in appreciation, he and Annie had been invited to an all-expense paid trip to view them at the Victoria and Albert Museum in London.

Charles remembered Annie telling him about how much she enjoyed the full English breakfasts there. Leaving Gretchen at home with the television set tuned to a children's cartoon channel, he drove the couple to The Acorn and Thistle, a quaint restaurant and tearoom near his home.

"This is wonderful," Annie said as she bit into a toasted, crunchy crumpet, dripping with honey and butter.

She took a sip of tea. "I got hooked on PG Tips when we were in England, and, as you are aware, it's become my drink of choice almost every morning. Thank you so much for bringing us here."

"I know you seemed bemused by our little spat yesterday, Charles, but I apologize again," Ed said. "The museum is a gem, and we shouldn't have been talking about the murder there."

Annie rolled her eyes. "Charles said he didn't mind, Ed. Can you get over it?"

"Ed, it's quite all right. Sometimes it makes sense to deal with a situation head on."

Soon after, they picked up Gretchen and headed back to Lighthouse Cove. Annie refused to concede that it had been inappropriate to bring up the murder case, then they decided to drop it and discussed other things. They agreed that their argument yesterday notwithstanding, their brief visit with Charles had been a nice respite and they were delighted and reassured to see their old friend so healthy.

Chapter 38

When Ed called Carrie on Monday, she concurred with Annie that Robert and Steven Swain should be interviewed. She knew the odds were slim that they were the killers, but the investigators had been running into brick walls with previous persons of interest; she figured it couldn't hurt.

She decided to not do a background check. The men had been part of the community for years, and Lighthouse Cove was so small that if either of them had gotten into trouble with the law, they'd have heard about it. Brad contacted them to request they come in for a quick chat. When they arrived, they were visibly nervous but after several minutes, relaxed.

He first asked if they might be related to a Swain family from South Carolina. They replied that to their knowledge they were directly descended from a man named Albert Swain, an indentured servant whose English master had conscripted him to fight in the War of 1812. They had learned through family lore that he was captured and imprisoned in Lighthouse Cove but had been treated so well by the Americans that he decided to remain there after the Treaty of Ghent was signed.

Steering the conversation to Citizens for Progress, he asked for an update. They said they weren't getting much interest but were hoping that calling attention to the fact that so many properties were off the tax rolls in Lighthouse Cove would result in some changes. They realized that instead of trying to strongarm people, they might need to change their tactics.

Brad asked where they'd been the day of Alex's murder; they replied they'd been in Buffalo and had spent the night with a cousin. They provided proof with receipts from an EZ Pass account and credit cards, and later, when Brad called him, the cousin verified the brothers' alibis.

That evening, while having their nightly glasses of wine before dinner Ed apprised Annie of Brad's interview with the Swains.

"They're in the clear, Annie. Their family came to this area during the War of 1812, and their alibis checked out."

"Could they have ordered a hit?"

Ed sputtered with laughter. "A hit? You mean as in mob-related?"

"I don't know. Maybe."

"Did you hear what I just told you? There's no motive, and Brad said they seemed genuinely sorry about the mayor's death. You don't like their politics so you're looking to pin something on them. There's no probable cause for us to investigate them further."

"It has nothing to do with politics, Ed; I told you I wasn't concerned about that."

She sighed. "I know they didn't kill Alex and expect you and Carrie were humoring me when you agreed they should be interviewed. I guess I was grasping at straws because I want so badly for Alex's killer to be apprehended. Still, every time I hear the name Swain it triggers something in my brain, and I feel discomfited. I just can't figure out why."

Realizing he'd been particularly hard on his wife, Ed apologized. "I know you cared for Alex and want his murder to be solved."

"I did, and I do. He helped write the grant that enabled us to undertake this project; he and I worked side-by-side on curating the exhibit, and he was a calm, supportive influence on my board. I miss him and am sick about his death. I have no idea why I'm fixated on the Swains, Ed, maybe it's just because I'm looking for monsters in closets when there aren't any."

They sat quietly for several minutes, each reflecting on the conversation. Ed broke the silence.

"Annie, I forgot to tell you that when Carrie, Brad and I spoke earlier today, we decided to take a break from the investigation for a few weeks. We're hoping a little distance from the case will bring clarity and help us look at it with a fresh perspective."

"I'm not surprised, Ed. I expect as in past cases, you'll eventually solve Alex's murder. Taking some time away is a good idea."

"I didn't schedule any other consulting jobs between Christmas and New Year's and wouldn't mind getting away for a few days. How would you feel about flying to Tampa and spending a few days in St. Pete's Beach? I know how you love the Gulf Coast."

"I do love the Gulf, Ed, but remember how crowded Florida was when we took the family on the Disney cruise a few years ago after Christmas? I expect St. Pete's Beach won't be quite as busy, but still there will be lots of parents taking their children to visit their grandparents; besides, it's not always warm there in December.

"Instead, how about if we go to Charleston? I expect there will be crowds, but maybe fewer than in Florida, and the temperature will be about the same as St. Pete's Beach. I'd like to visit the Swain Plantation. I discovered it's being run as a living history museum that contrasts the opulent lifestyle of the owners with the depravation of the slaves. Learning that Betsey Cooper had been enslaved there has piqued my interest, and I'd like to see if I can find more information about her."

"That would be fun, Annie. Let's plan to leave the Wednesday after Christmas and fly back on New Year's Day. I'll call Sandy and if she can watch Gretchen, I'll work on getting us airline tickets and a hotel."

Chapter 39

The Holiday Festival of Lights was held in the park next to the museum the following Saturday evening and started at dusk. Tall stadium field lights provided illumination, and the museum staff and volunteers had strung multi-colored holiday lights on bushes and around tree trunks. Several portable fire pits had been placed at strategic spots near park benches to provide warmth.

The Neighborhood Association maintained a booth that offered free hot chocolate and cookies. Other booths, with representatives from local Christian, Jewish, Muslim, and Hindu congregations, offered information about their holiday customs including the significance of light, and samples of traditional holiday food.

Santa ambled through the crowd passing out wrapped red and white candy. A group from near Tug Hill had brought live reindeer, tame enough to pet. Children hopped on the back of a fire truck, a huge wreath on its hood, for a ride around the block, speakers blaring seasonal winter songs.

A lighted Christmas tree had been erected in the middle of the park, a Chanukah menorah, Kwanzaa kinara, and clay diyas—oil lamps representing the Hindu holiday of Diwali—flanked the tree on large tables on either side.

Towards the end of the evening, the high school student chorus handed out sheets for a sing-along and led the community in a diverse selection of melodies representing all the groups at the festival.

Carrie attended with her family but took some time away from them to walk through the crowd with Mia. She was pleased there were no issues, and no sign of the Swains or their group of followers.

Chapter 40

Ed spent the next day sanding down the antique wardrobe, putting the porch furniture into the shed for winter, and cleaning the basement—another chore long overdue.

Instead of volunteering at the hospital, Annie was spending the day at the park with a group of volunteers, cleaning up from the festival. By late afternoon, awaiting her return, Ed took a container of curried spinach dip from the refrigerator and toasted and cut rounds of whole grain pita into wedges.

Tired and unenthusiastic about walking Gretchen, he let her out in the backyard after he fed her. She came back inside quickly—it had started to snow. Within minutes, she was sound asleep on her bed in front of the fire in the living room, snoring softly.

He poured himself a scotch, lit a fire in the fireplace, put a Christmas CD in the player, and sat in his recliner. Within a few minutes, he was fast asleep. Half an hour later, Annie came bouncing into the room, startling him awake. He yawned, stood up and kissed her. "What's making you so cheery on this snowy evening?"

"I just picked up our mail from yesterday. We were so busy I guess we both forgot to get it." She held a card out to him. He read it and grinned. "Well, good for him!"

The card announced the engagement of Jon Bradford to Stephanie Morris. Several years earlier, Ed, with Annie's help, had solved the murder of Jon's wife, Emily. Since then, the art dealer and the DeCleryks had become friends. They missed Emily but were pleased Jon had found someone to share his life with.

"As you read, Ed, they are having a small engagement party at the gallery the first weekend in January. I'd love to go, but we probably should consider spending the night. We have no idea what the weather will be like, and we'll be able to have a couple drinks and not be concerned about driving back here after the party."

"Let's make it a mini vacation. We can drive in early, go to a museum and have lunch at one of the museum cafés," Ed suggested. "I'll check and see if the B&B a few doors down from the gallery has any rooms available. That way we can park the car there and walk to the party."

"Great idea. I'll call Sandy and see if she can keep Gretchen overnight. I'm excited about this. Stephanie is a delightful woman and such a good fit for Jon. I'm so happy they've invited us."

He smiled. "So, does this mean a shopping trip to the mall for something to wear?"

Annie laughed. "I don't think so this time, Ed. As you read, cocktail attire is preferred. I have a few things in my closet that would be suitable and plenty of festive jewelry and shoes to go with whatever I decide to wear. Thanks, though, for suggesting it."

Just then the phone rang. It was Suzanne. She and Garrett had received the same invitation to the engagement party and were planning to attend. She invited Annie and Ed to spend the night with them at their condo in Rochester. Annie declined, saying that they wanted to have some romantic alone time. The friends spoke for a few minutes more, then ended the conversation.

Ed asked, "Can I pour you a glass of wine, Annie? I can open that Cab you enjoy. There's a bowl of leftover spinach dip you made yesterday with pita on the table. Did you plan anything for dinner? If not, we can go out."

"I was so busy today that I didn't even think about dinner. It's snowing hard right now, I'd rather stay in. We have some lentil soup in the freezer; I can defrost it in the microwave and make a salad. With the dip and pita, we won't end up hungry."

Chapter 41

Happy to have some time off work, Ed and Annie prepared for their annual Christmas Eve open house. After days of decorating, cooking, baking, and stocking the liquor cabinet and wine cellar, they finally felt ready to usher in the holiday with their friends and family.

They had invited Eve and Henri Beauvoir for a drink before the festivities began. When they arrived, the two couples greeted one another with hugs and shortly after, with beverages in hand, entered Ed's study.

After a few minutes of small talk, Eve said, "We have good news to share."

"What would that be?" Ed asked.

"Remember when we had dinner together at The Brewery in November, and we told you we were thinking about moving back to the village? We bought Lainie and Gabe Spurling's house; it's only a block from you."

Annie beamed. "That's wonderful! We'll be neighbors."

"The house is perfect for us. As you know, it's on one floor, and we're excited that we'll be able to walk to the beach, shops, and restaurants."

"Lanie was pregnant when they bought the house," Annie remarked. "They've only been there a couple years. It's adorable; why did they sell?"

"She's pregnant again; they're having twins. With only two bedrooms, the house is way too small. They're moving to a larger home on Hydrangea Lane."

"I don't remember seeing a For Sale sign."

"There was no sign; it was just listed. We finally made the decision to sell the house on White Pelican Island and contacted Shelley Carpenter at Cove Real Estate to get an idea of what our house would be worth when she told us about it. We made an offer the same day."

"Who was their listing agent?"

"His name is Josh Ward."

Ed shook his head, "Name's not familiar."

Annie replied, "His name is familiar to me, I can't remember where I would have heard it. Anyway, I'm delighted for you, and we'll love having you as neighbors."

By now, the other guests had started arriving; Annie and Ed excused themselves to greet them in the foyer where a quartet from the high school orchestra was playing selections from *The Nutcracker*.

Each room in the spacious home had been decorated with garlands of fresh greenery, berries and small, twinkling white lights. A ten-foot Balsam fir with ornaments collected from their first year of marriage took center stage in the high-ceilinged living room in front of a bank of French doors that opened onto their back porch and faced the lake.

Smaller decorated trees greeted visitors in the den and Ed's study. Fireplaces in each of the rooms were lit with applewood logs that crackled and danced, perfuming each room with a sweet and smoky scent.

The capacious dining room table groaned with food. A sideboard held trays of cookies and other desserts. A large rectangular table, replete with punch bowls of eggnog, Wassail, non-alcoholic punch, and a fully stocked bar, had been set along a wall in the den.

Annie and Ed's children and grandchildren were spending the night and, after their guests had left, helped to clean up, with the family finally retiring, exhausted but happy, at midnight.

On Christmas morning, Annie baked the sticky buns that had been rising in the refrigerator overnight—a family tradition. The adults drank cups of steaming coffee and spicy chai tea while the grandchildren drank hot chocolate and opened presents.

Chapter 42

A few days later, Ed and Annie boarded a plane at the Frederick Douglass Greater Rochester International Airport and flew to Charleston. Ed had booked a room at The Middleton, an elegant hotel located in the heart of the historic district. After landing, they picked up their rental car, drove to the hotel and checked in. An hour later and after grabbing sandwiches and drinks from a food truck, they strolled a few blocks to board a horse drawn carriage for a tour of the colorful antebellum homes of Rainbow Row.

By now it was late; they were tired and decided to eat dinner at the hotel's outdoor café. Annie was impressed with the lush beauty of its gardens, and both she and Ed admitted they were enjoying the balmier weather. Within minutes, a server appeared to take their drink orders, and over a single malt scotch for Ed and a Chardonnay for Annie, they perused the menu, settling on the Low Country fare for which the restaurant was famous.

The sun was setting, and dusk cast a purple haze above them. Multiple strands of globe string lights had been hung above the patio, creating the warm, romantic feel of an intimate French sidewalk café. White fairy lights woven through hedge rows of vivid crepe myrtle twinkled and danced in the light breeze that had tiptoed in with encroaching night. Servers, wearing white shirts and black pants, scurried around to turn on tall gaslit heaters as the temperature dropped and the air cooled. Annie, prepared, had brought a warm shawl that she draped around her shoulders; Ed was in shirt sleeves.

"I was thinking we could take a walk after we finish here," he said to her. "First, I'll need to go back to the room for a sweater. I'm getting a bit cold." He stood and pushed his chair in.

In an exaggerated Scarlett O'Hara accent, Annie drawled, "Oh my, that's just dreadful, you poor boy." Then she smiled. "I believe I can find a way to warm you up if you're willin' to forego our stroll."

Twirling the left side of an imaginary mustache and combining two of Rhett Butler's most famous lines in the movie, *Gone with the Wind,* Ed drawled, "Frankly my dear… you deserve to be kissed by someone who knows how to do it." He bent down and gently kissed her on the lips.

Annie laughed and, taking him by the hand, walked into the hotel. They entered their room, Ed closed the door and they kissed again, this time like the young lovers they once had been, the years melting away like snow under a bright morning sun.

Chapter 43

The next morning, Annie purchased a couple of regional cookbooks and some colorful linen napkins at City Market, the historic merchandise exchange that spanned several blocks in the heart of Old Towne. They boarded a boat to tour The Battery, visited the Slave Market Museum and drove to Folly Beach to walk the length of the pier that stretched more than 1,000 feet into the ocean. That night, they dined on shrimp and grits at a vernacular shotgun house that had been converted into a restaurant.

Energized and enjoying the sunshine and warm weather, they hopped in the car the following morning and drove to Morris Island Lighthouse, built in 1876. After that, they stopped at a museum to view the Hunley, a Confederate submarine that had disappeared in Charleston Harbor in 1864 with eight men aboard and had been discovered, intact, 136 years later. Ready to quit for the day, they drove back to the hotel and ordered room service for their dinner, enjoying the view of the gardens from their balcony as they ate.

On the last day of their trip, they visited the Swain Plantation. The columned mansion, restored to its original splendor, appeared like a phoenix rising out of the ashes at the end of a mile-long driveway paved with crushed oyster shells and lined with ancient live oak trees.

They parked in a nearby lot and purchased tickets at a booth that was a five-minute walk to the mansion. As soon as they entered, the first thing they saw along one wall in the foyer was an engraved plaque with the names—including Betsey's—of the enslaved people who had made the grandeur possible.

There was also a list of Swain family members along with copies of old photos, but there was no way to tell if one of the children was the offspring of Betsey and the plantation owner. They'd probably never learn why Betsey had been sent to work in the fields after serving so many years as a house slave, but when Annie questioned a docent, she speculated that perhaps as Betsey matured and became more beautiful, the plantation master's wife might have contrived to send her from the mansion house, knowing what would happen to her if she stayed.

The couple was shocked at the deplorable living conditions of the slave quarters while walking through the graveyard. So many had died in infancy and childhood or had not lived past their teens. The graveyard for the wealthy plantation owners and their families told a completely different story. Other than an occasional death of a woman who had died in childbirth or a baby who had been stillborn, most lived well into their 70s and 80s.

Annie had expected to learn more about Betsey Cooper and was disappointed that there were no additional records about what happened to her before she fled to Macyville. And while she knew the Swains hadn't killed Alex and weren't related to the people who owned the plantation, there was still something about the name that bothered her.

That night, Ed and Annie dined in the hotel's upscale restaurant, The Grille Room, which specialized in French/Southern cuisine. They were asleep before fireworks erupted over the harbor at midnight and flew home the next morning.

Chapter 44

New Year's Day was quiet and relaxing for the Ramos family. They watched the Rose Bowl parade, played board games, and had an early dinner of spaghetti and meatballs. By 7:30 that night, the children were tucked away in their beds. Matt turned the TV on to PBS and started watching a program on *Masterpiece Theater*. Carrie ambled into her study, turned on her computer and started surfing law enforcement sites.

As she'd promised her husband, she had visited her family doctor. He found her healthy except for a mild case of anemia, and he prescribed a low dose of iron. He agreed that she might still be suffering from postpartum depression and suggested a therapist who, after a few sessions, encouraged her to find other employment if she couldn't find a way to balance her family life with her job.

She discovered an online newsletter that posted positions in her field. The local community college needed a part-time instructor to work a couple nights a week teaching classes on investigative techniques. She dismissed that. She didn't want to work nights, although part-time work wouldn't be so terrible.

Rochester Institute of Technology had an open tenure track position in the Criminal Justice Department. She'd received her masters' degree from that department and believed she might be qualified to teach there. She printed off the information.

The Rochester Police Academy was searching for a full-time trainer to work from 8:30-5:00, five days a week with weekends off. The pay was good, benefits excellent; she printed off that information, too.

Other jobs would require relocating, and she dismissed those. She loved living in Lighthouse Cove, Matt was happy with his work, and their children were thriving. They had a good support system and moving elsewhere would only exacerbate her stress.

Shutting down her computer, she placed the job information in the top drawer of her desk and joined Matt. She'd wait until the next day to start completing applications and making phone calls.

Chapter 45

At 10:00 on January 2, after Ed left for a meeting with the police chief in Wolcott who wanted to hire him to do some diversity training for new recruits, Annie headed to the museum.

The sun was shining, the sky a brilliant robin's egg blue. White waves on a calm lake slapped gently onto shore, and the snow from earlier storms had melted. Although the morning was chilly, by mid-afternoon the temperature was supposed to rise to the mid-40s.

Except for some landscaping and last-minute additions to the buildings, the restoration project at Macyville was almost completed. Annie decided that it was a perfect day to visit the site, and asked Jason to join her, indicating it might also be a good day to have their celebratory lunch. She called The Brewery to make a reservation, but it was closed until dinner; instead, they decided to go to Bistro Louise.

At Macyville, for security, a rope was tied to two stakes driven into the ground across from each other with *No Trespassing* signs at either end. When they arrived at the settlement, the rope had been moved, and as they pulled into the parking lot, they noticed a black truck parked there.

"Construction workers?" Jason asked.

"I wasn't aware they were working today, Jason," Annie replied. "If they are, we'll remind them to secure the rope after they enter the premises.

"This is the second time this has happened in the past several weeks. The last time I visited, the ropes were also down. There's liability for us if anyone trespasses and is injured, plus we want to discourage vandals. I'll call the foreman and remind him to be more careful."

"That rope isn't going to discourage trespassers, Annie. If you want better security, you should have the contractors erect two locking swing gates across the entrance."

"You're right, Jason," Annie replied. "That's what was originally planned, but those gates are expensive. I figured that a rope across the entrance and the signs would discourage curiosity seekers. If this continues, we may have no choice. Let's go in and look around."

The visitors' center was steps from the parking lot. Glass paneled garage doors in the front and back of the stone building could be opened to catch the breezes when the weather permitted, and on the side facing inward towards the buildings, visitors could enjoy beverages and snacks under umbrellaed tables on a flagstone patio.

Annie punched a code into a keypad affixed to a wooden panel door on the north side, and the two entered the building. In a few months, the center would house a ticket booth, restrooms, a gift shop and in the middle of the large space, a glass case on a table with a miniature replica, built to scale, of the settlement.

The walls had been painted soft grey. Along one hung a thick plaster bas relief sculpted by a local artist that depicted Freedom Hill, figures running to the beach below, and a schooner—sails unfurled—waiting for them out on the water.

The exhibit at the museum would be moved permanently to a hall attached to the visitor's center. Beyond the building were the homes, the Friends' meeting house, a one-room schoolhouse, and businesses looking as though they had always been there.

"Oh, my!" Annie said with tears in her eyes. "Sorry, Jason, I didn't know I'd be this emotional. The contractors have done such a good job. I'm just so sad that Alex isn't around to see this."

"You worked hard on this, Annie. You should feel proud," Jason responded.

"You deserve credit, too, Jason. You've been a huge help in getting this off the ground.

"Let's check out the rest of the property," Annie suggested, wiping her eyes. They had just started walking through the settlement when they spied two men wandering around, taking photos with their cell phones.

Chapter 46

Annie shouted, "Excuse me!"

Startled, the men began to walk hurriedly toward the entrance. Annie and Jason intercepted them. They were wearing jeans, boots, peacoats and black watch caps; both wore sunglasses. One man was as tall as Ed; the other, several inches shorter.

Annie asked, "What you are doing here? Didn't you see the *No Trespassing* signs?"

The taller man replied, "Sorry. We're visiting the area and drove by the entrance and we were curious; we decided to check it out. We didn't think anyone would mind. What is this place? It's fascinating."

Impatient for the men to leave, Annie introduced herself and Jason and briefly explained the project. Something about them seemed vaguely familiar, and she thought she recognized their voices. She asked, "Have we met?"

The shorter one quickly replied "No, I'm sure we haven't."

"Why were you taking photos?"

The taller one answered, "We thought our wives would enjoy seeing these buildings, maybe we can come back when this opens to the public. Do you know when that will be?"

"If you have business cards, I'll add your contact information to our mailing list. Then you'll get announcements about our grand opening, which will be held July 4 weekend, and programs we'll be offering. Our brochure isn't ready yet; I can send you one when it's printed." Annie was hoping to learn their names.

"No cards," the taller one responded. "Do you have a website? I'm a history buff and would like to learn more about this place."

"We do." Annie reached into her coat pocket. "Here's my card; it has the website address on it, and if you email me, I'll put you on our mailing list. You're still not off the hook about the trespassing."

The men apologized again and ambled slowly toward the parking lot with Annie and Jason trailing behind them, watching closely as they drove away.

"Annie, do you think they were telling the truth? You know you've received calls from developers who are interested in purchasing part of the property near Freedom Hill. Could these men have lied to you and were here to surveil the place and then try to pressure you to sell it to them?"

"I hope not, Jason. I've made it clear to any developer or realtor who calls that we are unable to sell. When The Nature Conservancy deeded the property to us after we received the grant from the National Trust, we signed a legally binding document mandating that it must remain an historic site or for nature conservancy in perpetuity."

Chapter 47

Tables for two with views of the lake were filled with customers when Annie and Jason arrived at the Bistro. They were seated in the front of the restaurant at a four-top with a view of the street and across it, the bay, where a couple of small fishing boats chugged by. Annie shivered.

"I know perch is in season right now, but I certainly wouldn't want to be fishing on that bay today; it must be terribly cold," she remarked.

Jason, who'd been texting his girlfriend, looked up quickly and sheepishly grinned. "Sorry, Annie, I wasn't paying attention. I was texting Rachel."

Annie smiled. "Well, I guess that's important, too. How are things going?"

He'd just started to answer when Terri showed up at their table. Today she was all business, not seeming to have time for chitchat.

"Do you need menus?" she asked, as she gestured to the blackboard against one wall. "The specials are there. If you need some time, I'll come back later."

"I know what I'm having," Annie responded. "I'd like a bowl of the lobster bisque with a sour dough roll, plain. In addition to a glass of water, could you also please bring me a cup of Earl Grey tea, as soon possible. We were just at the Macyville site, and even though it's mild for January, I'm a bit chilled."

Terri cocked an eye at Jason. "You?"

"I'll have the turkey panini, a side of fries and a cola. You can bring my drink when you bring Annie's tea."

Terri nodded and turned toward the kitchen to place the order. Annie was about to say something to Jason about Terri's chilly reception when the door opened, and Ed and Brad entered the restaurant. Annie smiled when she saw her husband and waved. He grinned and waved back.

"Come and join us!" Annie called out. "We just ordered lunch."

The men made their way over to the table, pulled out two chairs and sat down. "I got back from Wolcott a little while ago and stopped by the station to check in with Carrie. Brad was walking into the building as I was leaving. I thought it might be nice for us to have a leisurely lunch together," Ed said.

"We asked Carrie to join us, but she said she wants to contact the media again to ask that they put the word out that the police department is still looking for tips from anyone who might know anything or have seen anything related to Alex's murder."

"I hope that results in some solid leads, Ed. It's time for this case to be closed."

Terri came back and took the two men's orders, this time ignoring Brad. While they waited for their food, Annie summarized their trip to Macyville and about the men who were trespassing.

"You sound alarmed, Annie. Was there something about them that concerned you?"

"I don't know. They were perfectly pleasant but seemed guarded, and even though they denied it, I feel as if I've met them before; their voices certainly sounded familiar. I couldn't get them to give me their names.

"I guess I'm just frustrated, I wish people would respect *No Trespassing* signs. I understand they were curious about the site and probably had no intention of disturbing anything. Still, it was disrespectful, plus, if one of them had tripped over construction materials and been hurt, there might have been a liability issue.

"Jason suggested we have the construction workers erect gates with a lock at the entrance, but that's going to cost more money than we have right now. Instead, I'll call the foreman and ask if he can dig through the permafrost and put some concrete stanchions in the ground and place a heavy metal chain across them with a keypad lock.

"It won't stop people on foot from getting into the site, but it would make it difficult for vehicles. If that doesn't work, then I suppose the next step would be to find the money to purchase the gates. We're so close to finishing the project, we don't want to encourage vandalism."

As they'd been talking, Terri arrived with their beverages, and then their meals.

Annie thanked her and looked at her companions. "Enough talk about Macyville. Let's enjoy our lunches."

Chapter 48

Carrie hoped her phone calls to the media would generate some tips, realizing she'd have to sift through a myriad of ones that had no merit. She expected some to be of sightings of flying saucers carrying Alex into the heavens, or someone who saw someone shoot a man two hours south of Lighthouse Cove that same morning, believing he'd been transported back to Lighthouse Cove in an armored tank. Or maybe someone would report that Alex wasn't dead, that he'd been seen walking a dog in Ithaca. That was par for the course. Interspersed with the crazy ones, she hoped that someone would come forward with knowledge about who had committed the crime.

She checked her personal email account. She had sent off resumes to the community college, the Police Academy, and R.I.T. So far, no one had responded; she remained hopeful. She had pretty much decided to resign as police chief by the end of the year.

Placing her head down on her desk, she sighed. She had loved being chief-of-police, yet she felt completely burned out and unable to continue. Managing a stressful job along with raising a family just wasn't working for her. She was wracked with guilt, when she was at work because she wasn't at home, and also when she was at home because she wasn't focusing on the job. Unless some sort of miracle happened, her only option would be to find a job with regular hours.

Her cell phone rang; she didn't recognize the caller ID. She answered, "Lighthouse Cove Police Chief, Carrie Ramos, how can I help you?"

The caller was the commander of the police academy. She'd received the resumé Carrie had emailed, and as it turned out, they were interested in interviewing her for the position, which would start in the fall.

Carrie hadn't expected her job search to bear fruit so quickly or be so easy, and her heart pounded with anticipation and a little dread. If she followed up with an interview and got the job, would she have second thoughts come fall?

She scheduled the interview, hoping that if she were offered the position and decided to take it, she might still have time to solve the murder case before she left the police force.

Hanging up the phone, she noticed Ed standing in her doorway.

"I know you didn't want to join Brad and me for lunch, so I brought you something. You need to take care of yourself, Carrie." He placed a cup of mocha latte and a chicken salad sandwich on a brioche roll on her desk.

"Thank you, Ed." Her eyes gleamed with appreciation and brimmed with the beginning of what appeared to be tears.

"Carrie, what's bothering you? You haven't been yourself for ages."

"Please sit down, Ed. If you have time, I'll tell you what's going on with me."

Carrie explained how she was feeling about the job, and the call she'd had for an interview at the police academy.

"If I leave, would you be willing to serve as interim police chief, Ed? Brad isn't qualified yet, and I expect the mayor and trustees would be delighted to have you come back, even if it's for a short time while they conduct a national search."

"Not going to happen, Carrie. I'm happy working part-time as a criminal consultant. It gives me time to do other things. Are you certain you want to leave?"

"No, but I feel I have no other options."

"If you didn't have so many other responsibilities and commitments, would you still want to leave?"

Carrie shook her head. "I love this job and would stay here until retirement if I could."

"Your children won't be small forever, Carrie. Maybe there's some way you can get through this rough period without quitting."

"I don't know how that will be possible."

"You're good at brainstorming. I've seen how well you do when we've investigated other murders together. Take some time to write down solutions that would enable you to stay in the job."

"I've already done a little of that, Ed. Matt and I discussed hiring a nanny or au pair, either option is expensive. Plus, we don't have room in the house for live-in help, and a nanny could decide to leave at any time. I don't want my children to be raised by someone they barely know. Those options are out."

"I expect there are solutions to your situation, Carrie. You just haven't thought of them yet."

Chapter 49

Brad was writing a traffic accident report when Carrie entered his office.

"I just got a call from a woman who lives near the high school. There was an early dismissal today, and a group of students have congregated across the street from her house. The school buses have already left. She has no idea why the students weren't on them unless they were walking home or had after school plans. She believes there's trouble brewing, some sort of argument between two of them that she fears is starting to escalate. She requested we check it out before it becomes violent."

"Isn't that normally something the school district would handle?"

"Yes, but it's not on school property and because a neighbor called it in, you'll need to be involved. Normally, I'd send Mia, but as you know, she's been working night shift the past few months because she's taking day classes at R.I.T. for her master's degree in criminal justice."

When Brad arrived at the scene, several students had crowded around two young men and were attempting to pull them apart. As he got out of his car and closer to the group, he recognized Billy Cooper as one of the fighters. He didn't recognize the other boy. As soon as the others noticed the detective, they backed away.

"What's going here?" he asked.

No one answered. "Billy? Can you explain to me why you were fighting?"

The teenager shrugged. "He started it. He called me stupid because I didn't do well on our history test."

"Why didn't you just ignore him?"

"I'm not stupid. I just decided not to study for the test. He did it to provoke me, and I couldn't let it pass."

Brad looked at the other boy, who hung his head. "What's your name? Did you do what Billy said?"

"I'm Trevor Wellington. I know Billy is smart, but the test wasn't hard, so I was ribbing him about not passing it. We've been friends for a long time, and I didn't expect him to hit me." He looked at Billy. "Sorry, man." Billy looked away.

"I could take you both back to the station and charge you with assault, but instead we're going to get into my car, and then I'm going to call your parents."

Trevor's father was an attorney whose office was a few blocks from the school. Within minutes, he came and got his son, indicating that he would face consequences at home.

Greg Cooper was at a finance committee meeting at his church when Brad called him. He was aware of the early dismissal. Billy was supposed to walk over to the church and after the meeting ended, he'd planned on taking him shopping for sneakers. He said he would call Laura and asked Brad to bring Billy home and wait for them.

The detective pulled into the driveway of the Victorian home that was located across the street from the museum. Painted pale yellow with salmon and green trim, it had a wide, wraparound porch with an attached gazebo on the north side. A separate carriage house at the end of the driveway had been converted to a garage.

Greg arrived first, Laura minutes later. They invited Brad inside and sent Billy to his room, a discussion of his punishment to be determined later.

Perching on the edge of a green velvet wing chair across the matching sofa where Brad and Greg sat in the spacious living room, Laura said, "Since earlier in the fall after he got caught breaking into the cars, Billy's grades have fallen; he's sullen and belligerent, won't attend scout meetings and we're practically dragging him to church on Sundays."

"Any problems here at home?" Brad asked.

The couple looked at each other. Greg answered. "No. Laura and I are fine. We're okay financially, nothing's changed. We'd like to think this is normal adolescent rebellion, but it seems more than that. We asked the school guidance counselor to speak with him, but he missed the appointment. Said he didn't need to talk with anyone."

"Do you have any idea what's going on?"

Laura sighed. "None. We're stumped. We've told him we love him and that he can talk with us about anything, and we won't judge him. He simply won't engage. He denies it's because he's still grieving for Alex."

"I'm reluctant to even bring this up, but is there any possibility he could have been molested or bullied without your knowing about it? Could he have started using drugs?"

"No, not that we're aware of, and we keep a close eye on him as we did with his sister before she left for college. Our son is vehemently anti-drug, and up until recently, our relationship with him has been so open and trusting that we're certain he'd speak with us if he felt threatened in any way. We're terrified that for whatever reason, he's on a downward slide and we're not sure what to do about it."

"How about some counseling for yourselves to help figure out how to deal with Billy?" Brad suggested.

"That's a good suggestion, detective," Greg Cooper responded. "We'll call and make some inquiries; hopefully, we can find someone who will see us quickly so we can help our son."

Laura thanked Brad for bringing Billy home and told him that after he left, they were going to go upstairs to his room and speak with him. Something was going on;

they prayed they could get to the bottom of it before it got worse.

Audio #4—Hiram Ward

Hiram Ward was born on a plantation in Georgia in 1830. When his mother, a house slave, died in 1843 he was sold to the Ward Plantation in Alabama where he became the personal servant to his master's young son and was permitted to join him for his lessons. His master had taken a liking to the affable young man and encouraged him to take on odd jobs to earn extra money. Seven years later, when he was 20, he purchased his freedom. Soon after, he fled to Macyville, fearing that even with a certificate of emancipation, he would be captured and forced back into slavery.

Within months of his arrival, he met a young woman named Clarice Macy. Clarice's pregnant mother had escaped to Macyville from a plantation in Virginia after the beating death of her husband, Moses. Within days of her arrival, she died of puerperal fever shortly after giving birth. Benjamin Macy and his wife adopted the baby and raised her with their three other children. Hiram and Clarice married in 1851 and were parents to Jeremiah, born in 1852; Ruth in 1853; Marigold, in 1855; Stella, in 1856; and Denis in 1858.

In late 1859, upon his return from his first trip across the lake with Samuel Weatherfield, Hiram, a newspaper reporter for the Silver Bay Times, *set up an interview with Abraham and Miranda Butler. Miranda noticed that the reporter bore a striking resemblance to her husband—he was of medium height, had curly dark hair, tawny skin, and green eyes. The two men exchanged remembrances of their childhoods and discovered they'd been born on the same plantation in Georgia: both offspring of the green-eyed plantation owner.*

On the next trip to Canada with Weatherfield, Hiram introduced himself to Betsey, who, like Abraham, was delighted to learn she had a half-sibling.

When the Civil War ended, Hiram and his family relocated to Ithaca, NY, where he had been hired as the editor of the News Journal. *From 1865 until his death from injuries sustained in a carriage accident in 1887, the Butler, Cooper and Ward families kept in close contact. After that, there are no records of a continued relationship between his family and the others.*

Chapter 50

The Saturday morning of the engagement party dawned clear and bright. It had snowed overnight, a fine powder that glinted and sparkled in the sun. After breakfasting in the heated sunroom adjoining their kitchen, Ed and Annie bundled up in warm clothing, donned their snow boots and took Gretchen, swathed in a quilted red coat, out for a walk.

Taking a route that led them past historic homes, some built before the War of 1812, they strolled along a path towards the municipal beach until they came to a parking lot piled high with mounds of snow that had accumulated over several weeks and had been deposited there by snow removal trucks. The snack bar and bathhouse were closed for winter. An adjacent pavilion stacked with picnic tables and a playground were just beyond it.

At the end of a long, stone pier, a white obelisk-shaped lighthouse, its red roof encasing a Fresnel lens, blinked off and on—a welcome and a warning to sailors at night. Gretchen, excited, pulled Ed, who was holding onto her leash, across the lot to the broad, wide beach. Then she stopped in her tracks and stared.

When the temperature had plummeted for several days, waves had crashed layer upon layer on the beach and frozen in place along the shoreline. Tinted a pale, translucent bluish green, the icy water absorbing the colorful rays of the sun, their jagged forms reminded Annie of miniature icebergs.

Stepping gingerly onto the snow-covered sand, Gretchen took a few steps, turned around to look at Ed and Annie, as if to say, 'I'm not doing this!" and hopped quickly on her front and back legs to them, then strained the leash towards the road.

Annie laughed. "She loves the snow, except when she doesn't. I guess we should head home."

Ed, who normally didn't feel the cold as much as Annie, was freezing.

"Let's stop at the Bistro for some hot chocolate and cookies. We can sit outside on the patio with Gretchen. They probably have the heaters on. Louise always has some of those homemade peanut butter dog bones, which should make our beagle happy."

"Good idea. We might as well enjoy the sun while it lasts; we know the unending grey days are coming soon."

Chapter 51

Several hours later, the pair were on their way to Rochester to meet Suzanne and Garrett at the Memorial Art Gallery for a tour of an Andy Warhol exhibit, on loan from the Bank of America. A couple hours later, they entered the Gallery's café and ordered a light lunch of homemade soup, salad, and bread, and shared a bottle of dry Rosé.

After lunch, their friends headed home; Ed and Annie drove to the B&B and checked in. Their cozy room had a warming fireplace, four-poster bed that sat atop a rose and teal Oriental rug, and two wing-backed chairs upholstered in burgundy velvet. The couple spent the afternoon dozing and reading; then Annie took a fragrant bubble bath in the capacious claw-foot tub; after that, Ed showered while she dressed for the evening.

At 7:00, Ed and Annie walked up four steps to the entrance of Gallery 21, a red-brick Federal-style building that nestled hip-to-hip with others on the tree-lined street. Annie had chosen to wear an ankle-length black velvet column dress with long sleeves, high-heeled black leather boots and sparkly jewelry. Ed wore a dark grey suit with a black cashmere mock turtleneck sweater. Annie remarked that with his white hair and deep blue eyes, he looked quite distinguished and handsome.

A young man dressed in black pants and a white shirt with a black bowtie opened the door, greeted them, took their coats, handed them each a glass of champagne, and ushered them into the building.

Inside, glossy black walls with white trim and polished pickled oak hardwood floors made a spectacular setting for the modern metal sculpture, black and white photos and glass bowls that had been placed strategically around the room.

Ed recognized Sophie, Jon's niece, a tall, slim redhead who stood with her arm around the waist of a tall, slim, blond man, whom Ed assumed was her husband, Hunter. Sophie and Ed hugged and introduced their spouses. Annie said she remembered meeting Sophie at Emily's funeral.

Ed asked the young woman if she were still working for Jon as his receptionist. A graduate of the Eastman School of Music, she and Hunter had been performing with a chamber music group allowing her to work at the gallery when there were no performances or practice sessions.

She beamed. "We both just got hired full-time with the Rochester Philharmonic. I play the cello and Hunter, the violin. Unfortunately, I don't have time to help Jon. He hired one of my friends, who's attending graduate school at Eastman."

Just then, another couple joined them. Ed and Annie greeted Sophie's parents whom they had also met at Emily's funeral, and the three couples spoke for a few minutes more.

The DeCleryks excused themselves, wandered into the gallery, then separated. Annie was standing in line waiting for a glass of wine, when she and the man behind her began to talk. He was as tall as Ed, but with a beefy build, dark hair, and a trim beard. He appeared to be in his 50s.

"Fun party," he said, then introduced himself. "I'm Frank Henderson"

Annie introduced herself and asked him how he knew Jon and Stephanie. He replied that he and his wife were antique dealers in Buffalo and that Stephanie rented the loft above their building for her studio.

"We've become quite good friends and will miss her when she moves here. We do plan to keep in touch. What about you?"

"I run the Lighthouse Cove Museum and Historical Society. Jon's former wife, Emily, was on my board of directors and ran our gift shop. My husband is a criminal consultant who investigated her murder and interviewed Jon after her death, and we became friends. We miss Emily terribly, but we're so happy he's found someone."

"I heard about her death. Tragic."

"It was horrible and senseless." She changed the subject. "Have you ever been to Lighthouse Cove? It's quite charming."

"As a matter of fact, my wife and I have. We met a couple, Ron and Chandra Fillmore, on a cruise a few years ago and became friendly with them. They live on the south shore in a house overlooking the bay. Do you know them?"

"I don't," Annie admitted.

"Last year we attended a picnic at their house on July 3 and stayed to watch the fireworks over the lake. It was spectacular."

"It is quite a show. We get a little more bang for our buck by having it a day before the official holiday and it gives our residents time to do other things on the 4th."

"We liked it so much we're considering purchasing some land to build a vacation home. Ideally, we'd like one with water access so we could have a dock and a boathouse. Are you aware of any property that's for sale?"

"I'm afraid there aren't many options, unless you want to build on one of the islands, but mainly those are accessible only by boat. If you want to stay on the peninsula, you'd certainly be able to purchase a home that's already been built with water access, but the only available building lots are near the golf course or in the woods between the bay and the lake. Neither development is on the water, although with some lots you might have a water view."

"When we were driving into the village last summer, we noticed construction trucks pulling into a site along the water a couple miles outside Lighthouse Cove. There are trees surrounding the property so we couldn't see what was being built, what about there?"

"The historical society owns that land. We acquired it from The Nature Conservancy a little more than a year ago." She explained about the Macyville project and how the land was zoned.

"That sounds like a fascinating project; once it's finished, my wife and I will make sure to plan a visit, but it's too bad at least part of it's not available for residential development. It looks like it would be a developer's dream."

"Believe me, I've had lots of calls from developers wanting to purchase the entire acreage or even a portion of it. They've been persistent, but again, that land is not for sale. If you call the Chamber of Commerce, they can give you a list of realtors who might be able to help you find what you're looking for." For some reason, the conversation discomfited Annie, but she couldn't figure out why.

A young man approached them with a tray of hors d'oeuvres. They declined and ended the conversation.

"Good luck with your house hunting," Annie said.

"And good luck to you with your project," replied Frank.

Annie found Ed, who was talking with Suzanne and Garrett and Jon and Stephanie, who said they would all receive an invitation to the wedding, which would be held in the gardens behind the gallery in late spring.

At 10:30, after thanking and saying good-bye to their hosts, Ed and Annie headed back to the B&B and by 11:30 were fast asleep.

Chapter 52

The next evening, Matt was in bed reading, and Carrie had just gone into the children's rooms for one last check when her phone buzzed. She sighed, thinking it was a robocall, then looked at her caller ID. It was Jake Corney, the police dispatcher.

"What's up, Jake?"

"Sorry to bother you, Carrie. I think you might want to take this one. I got a call from Greg Cooper. His son, Billy, is missing along with a gun and ammunition from his gun safe."

Carrie groaned. She was exhausted as usual. Natasha had been wound up for some reason and had difficulty settling down after she was put to bed, and Arturo had another ear infection and was fussy. The doctor had recommended putting drainage tubes in his ears to avoid repeat occurrences; they'd schedule that after the infection cleared.

"Thanks, Jake. Please call the Coopers and let them know I'll be there shortly."

Throwing on some clothes, she explained to Matt what was going on, and in fifteen minutes arrived at the Cooper house. Greg, dressed in jeans and a sweatshirt, was waiting for her on the porch; his wife, Laura, dressed in a robe and slippers, was pacing in the living room.

"Why would he do this?" Carrie asked, now sitting on the sofa with Laura, Greg nearby in a wingback chair.

Greg shrugged. "You know he's been difficult for weeks. First the car burglaries, and since then his grades have been slipping. He got into that fight at school. Even though he's denied it, we wondered if this acting out has something to do with Alex's death—our families were very close. When we asked him if he was still grieving, he said if he were, he'd be the only one in the family who was. I asked him why he believed that, and he shrugged.

"I explained that I was grieving, too, but showing it differently than he may have expected. I'm having trouble sleeping and difficulty concentrating. I said I feel sad almost all the time, but when I cry I do so in private. I reminded him that his mother and I have visited Cheryl several times to offer support and take meals to her. After that, he shook his head, said, 'yeah, right,' and walked away.

"We have no idea why he reacted the way he did, and why he's been so surly. As Detective Washington suggested, Laura and I visited a therapist to see if we could figure out how to help Billy. She offered to do a home visit and thought that if we could talk as a family in her presence, she might be able to learn what's going on with our son. When we find him, it's certainly worth trying."

Laura started to cry. Greg walked over to her and put his arm around her.

"I remember Detective Washington telling me that he'd asked if Billy could have been bullied or molested, and you responded that you keep a close eye on your children and had no evidence that anyone was harming him."

Neither parent could think of anything that might have happened to distress their son. There had been no signs of anything suspicious going on; they trusted the teachers and coaches at the school. Their minister was a 65-year-old grandmother who'd been with the church for 20 years, and Greg's brother, Bobby, was the youth advisor there. Greg added that Bobby was a decorated state policeman and Billy adored him.

"What happened tonight?"

Greg said, "Billy said he was going into our bonus room behind the garage to study for a test and then he planned to watch the rest of the Lakers game on TV. It should have been over about 10:00. Laura had already gone to bed, and I was locking up when I realized that Billy hadn't come back into the house.

"I thought maybe he'd fallen asleep and went to check on him. He was gone, the gun safe was open, and a revolver and ammunition were missing. It was my grandfather's gun; he was a sheriff in Ohio. It's in working order. I've never used it; I kept it for sentimental reasons."

"Are either of your cars missing? Carrie asked.

Greg and Laura shook their heads. "He didn't take a car, and his bike is still here. Wherever he is, he went on foot. We called his friends; no one has seen him."

"We'll start looking for him right away. There are a lot of woods, fields, and bluffs around here, so he could be anywhere. Hopefully, he's not planning to harm someone or himself. Stay by your phone and try to be optimistic."

Back in her car, Carrie called the county sheriff; within minutes several patrol cars had fanned out through the area looking for the missing boy. Unfortunately, six hours later, he was still missing, so they called off the search, deciding that they would resume it after sunrise. Carrie had a terrible sense of foreboding.

Chapter 53

With no possibility of sleep, Carrie went home, roused Matt, summarized what had occurred and said she was going to her office. He promised to wake and feed Natasha and Arturo and take them to daycare, indicating that he was concerned about her health and emotional state. She assured him she was fine.

No one else was in the building when she arrived; Carrie read her mail, worked on her report for the village trustees, and dozed off for an hour. At 7:00, she crossed the street to Bistro Louise for coffee and a pastry. The sheriff had called and said that his officers would take the lead in continuing to search for Billy Cooper that morning.

At 8:30, Ed rapped on Carrie's office door. She motioned for him to enter and told him about Billy Cooper's disappearance.

Ed thought for a moment. "Either something happened to Billy Cooper that he's reluctant to tell his parents about, or his family is hiding some deep secrets that he's no longer able to keep."

"You don't think he killed Alex, do you?"

"I can't imagine what his motive would be. Plus, he was on a field trip with his history class the day Alex was killed. They started out visiting abolition sites in Rochester in the morning, then after lunch came back here and went to the museum for a tour of the Macyville exhibit. Annie said Billy was particularly distraught when he heard the news about Alex."

"Still, I think we need to check it out," Carrie responded. "Depending on when the class left for the field trip, it would have been possible for him to meet Alex at the site first and then get to school in time to meet the others."

Carrie called the main number at the high school and asked to speak with the principal. After explaining the reason for her call, she was put on hold for several minutes. Shortly after, she gave a thumbs up to Ed, thanked the principal and hung up.

"He was late that day, for a legitimate reason. He had a dentist appointment at 7:30. He left the dentist at 8:30 with a written excuse, and walked back to school; it took him about 15 minutes. He arrived in time to board the bus with the others at 9:00. He remained with them for the rest of the day. We're back to square one.

"Let's hope we can find him before he harms himself. I'm going to call Brad and let him know what's going on."

Chapter 54

Ed riffled through a professional magazine on Carrie's desk while she called Brad. He'd been investigating a cash register robbery at a convenience store just outside the village; he said he was finishing up and would be back shortly. A couple minutes later, the intercom on her phone buzzed. She picked up the phone
"Yes?"
"It's Barb, Carrie. You have a visitor…Billy Cooper is here to see you."
Carrie took a sharp breath. "Is he okay?"
"He seems to be. He surrendered a revolver with a box of ammunition and asked to speak with you."
"Please escort him back here."
"Brad just arrived. Billy is with him."
A few seconds later, accompanied by Brad, Billy entered Carrie's office, green eyes wild and frantic.
"Billy, please tell us why you ran away. Your parents are beside themselves with worry, and we've had county sheriffs out for most of the night and this morning looking for you. You could have frozen to death. Where were you?"
"I started out in the woods behind our house trying to decide what to do. I got cold and needed a place where I could think things through so went to the cottage of a friend from sailing camp. It's located near the yacht club and the family uses it in the summer and on weekends and holidays. I know where the spare key is and let myself in. They keep the heat turned on low when they aren't there, I turned it up and found some food. I was perfectly comfortable and safe."
So, in addition to everything else Billy has done, we can add breaking and entering to the list. No wonder we couldn't find him, Carrie thought, *we were looking in all the wrong places.*

"We know you took your great-grandfather's revolver from your dad's gun safe. Why? I promise, we can help you."

"I took the gun because I thought about killing myself, but then I realized I could never do that, it would destroy my mom. That's when I was in the woods. I had time to think about what I wanted to do when I spent the night at my friend's house. I'm turning myself in. I'm confessing. I murdered Alex."

For several seconds the investigators were speechless, then Carrie said, "We know you were at the dentist early that morning and then took a field trip with your class. You couldn't have murdered Alex."

Billy refused to say more, and Carrie put him in an interview room with Brad until she could figure out what was going on. Something wasn't feeling right about his confession.

Carrie walked into her office and called the hardware store. The line was busy, so she called Laura Cooper who had taken the day off work and explained to her that Billy was safe but had confessed to murdering Alex.

Laura, relieved that her son was unharmed, responded that he was lying, but she had no idea why. He had no access to a car that day, she knew he hadn't taken his bike, and she verified that she'd dropped him off for a dentist appointment at 7:30 that morning, then he walked back to school in time to board the bus for the field trip. Their insurance paid for the dentist appointment, and she had the paperwork to prove it.

"Something else is going on, Carrie. I'm going to call Greg and we'll be at the police station shortly."

Carrie and Ed walked into the interview room. "Billy, the principal at your school and mother both verified that you were at a dentist appointment about the time Alex was killed, and then were with your history class the rest of the day."

"I killed Alex. I snuck out on my bike and met him at 6:30 at Freedom Hill and was back home in time for my mom to take me to the dentist."

"Is the revolver you turned in the one you used?"

"Yes."

"I don't know why you're lying, Billy, but Alex was at home talking to his wife at 6:30 the morning he was murdered, and a shotgun killed him. Are you covering for someone?"

Billy hung his head and remained silent, then he started crying.

"I can't take this anymore. I've been carrying it around for months. You're right, I didn't kill Alex, my dad did! He says he's sad about his death, but he's not, and I have proof."

Carrie said, "Your dad has an alibi."

"No, he doesn't. His employees lied for him. I was there, at the store, a little after 8:30 on my way back to school from the dentist appointment. He wasn't."

He explained. On the morning of the mayor's murder, he decided to stop at the hardware store on his way back to school from the dentist to tell his father he'd had two cavities filled and the claim would be submitted to the insurance company.

The dentist's office was a block away from the store, and he cut through the parking lot to enter through the back door. Greg's car wasn't there, but Billy thought maybe for some reason he'd parked out front. Once inside, he asked for his dad. The store manager said he'd gone to run an errand.

At that point, Billy thought nothing about it. That evening at dinner, his parents were talking about the murder. His mother said she expected the investigators would want to interview Greg and the rest of Alex's poker buddies since they were the last ones to see him alive before he was killed, not because they were suspects. She said she knew they had alibis. His father didn't refute her statement.

Billy kept quiet and didn't mention he'd visited the store; Greg's employees must have forgotten to tell his father that he'd been there after his appointment.

After dinner, Billy informed his parents that he was going to finish his homework and watch some sports on the big screen TV in the bonus room behind the garage. It was where his father kept his gun safe.

The safe was closed but not locked, which was highly unusual. He opened it; one shotgun was out of place. He smelled it. It had been recently fired. His dad had not, to his knowledge, gone hunting this season. They typically hunted together.

Then he figured it out. His dad must have killed Alex and hadn't had time to clean the gun and forgot to lock the case in his haste to get back to work that day. He was certain his dad had lied about his whereabouts that morning but was terrified to confront him.

"When my history class took the tour of the exhibit at the museum the afternoon that Alex was murdered, I listened to the audio descriptions about his family. I learned he was related to Abraham and Miranda Butler; his sister, Betsey, who married a man named William Cooper; and a half-brother, Hiram Ward. Betsey and her husband remained in Canada after the end of the Civil War, but some of their descendants eventually came back to the states. Many of the Macyville descendants, including Alex, have green eyes.

"My name is William Cooper. We have the same last name as Abraham's sister; my dad and I both have green eyes, and my dad has tawny skin. I think Alex may have discovered we were related. I guess my dad was okay having a friend with Black ancestors but didn't want anyone to know we do, too. He's such a hypocrite."

"That's why you'd been getting into so much trouble, isn't it? You're angry and scared." Carrie placed her hand on Billy's shoulder.

"I am. Alex and my dad were as close as brothers, at least I thought they were. My sister and I used to call him Uncle Alex until we got older. He and Cheryl and their children have been part of our family forever; we celebrated holidays together."

Carrie walked out of the room with Brad and called Laura Cooper while Ed stayed behind in the interview room.

"Hi, Carrie, we're on our way. Greg just stopped by the house to pick me up."

"I think it would be better if we met you at your home, Laura. We'll explain when we get there."

"I goofed, Carrie," Brad said. "When I called Greg's employees to check on his alibi all I asked is for them to confirm that Alex had opened the store that morning, believing that he'd been there all day. I didn't ask the right questions."

"Brad, one mistake isn't going to ruin your career, plus I'm not convinced Greg *is* our killer. I think something else is going on; let's go find out what it is."

Chapter 55

Brad retrieved the gun and ammunition, secured it in a locked closet for safekeeping and went back to his office to record some notes about the burglary. Ten minutes later, Carrie and Ed, with Billy in tow, arrived at the Cooper house. Laura Cooper was waiting for them and ushered them through the front door. When she saw her son, she put her arms around him and hugged him.

"Honey, why did you run away? We've been so worried about you. We thought something terrible had happened to you." The young man started crying.

"Where's Greg?" Carrie asked.

"He's in the kitchen getting a drink of water. He'll be back in a minute."

When Greg saw Billy, he hugged him and said, "Why did you run away? What's been troubling you? Has someone harmed you?"

Carrie looked at Billy. "Perhaps you can explain to your father why we're all here."

"Dad, I tried to keep it quiet. I was so angry I couldn't hold it in any longer."

"What in the world are you talking about?" his father asked.

"You did it, Dad; you killed Alex. Why do you think I've been so angry lately? I can't believe my own father would commit murder."

"What? Why ever would you think that? Alex was one of my best friends. We were like brothers."

Billy explained. Laura Cooper gasped.

Greg said, "We got busy later that morning; no one told me you'd stopped by on your way back to school from your dentist appointment. If they had, I might have been more forthcoming at dinner that night about my whereabouts, but you didn't say anything about it then, either.

"I didn't kill Alex, Billy, and I wish you'd talked with someone you trusted earlier so we could have cleared this up sooner."

He explained. He had opened the store at 7:00 on the day of the murder but when the investigators interviewed him and his friends, he didn't volunteer that he'd left the shop for a couple hours after that. He'd been having chest pains and shortness of breath. His father had died young from a heart attack, so he'd scheduled an appointment with a cardiologist. His staff agreed to cover for him.

"My doctor will vouch for me. I was in his office taking a battery of tests when you showed up at the store."

Laura looked stricken. "Why wouldn't you tell me?"

"I didn't want to scare you or Billy, just in case it was a false alarm, which it was. It turned out I was having some acid reflux problems; you've seen the prescription in the medicine chest, and I told you about *that*. I saw no reason to go into further detail. I'm fine."

He looked at his son, "I didn't lie to your mother, if you remember, I didn't respond at all, and I didn't lie to the police. No one asked if I had been at the store all day."

"Dad, I checked the gun safe that night. One of the shotguns had been used, and the safe was unlocked. How can I trust you?"

Greg, startled, said, "Oh my, no wonder you believed I killed Alex. I can explain. Doug Kilmer, one of the men in my church prayer group, borrowed it. He can vouch for me. His wife was pregnant with their first child, and she didn't want any guns around the house. I offered to let him keep his guns here. He responded that he wasn't going to do much hunting after the baby was born, he'd sold them.

"Then a couple of his friends asked if he wanted to go hunting; it was the day of Alex's murder. He still had his hunting license, and he called and asked if he could borrow one of mine. I gave him the combo to the keypad for the bonus room, we always keep it locked, and the combo to the lock on the gun safe. I asked that when he was finished, to clean the gun and return it, expecting we'd be home by then.

"He'd just shot off a couple rounds when his wife called. She'd gone into early labor and one of their neighbors was taking her to the hospital. He didn't want to leave the rifle in the car, so he brought it back here and put it in the safe. He didn't have time to clean it and in haste forgot to lock the safe and to tell me about it.

"I didn't go into that room until a few days later, the safe was locked. I guessed you locked it, son. I never checked to see if the gun had been cleaned, and I only discovered it wasn't a couple weeks later when I went to target practice with my poker buddies. I called Doug, and he apologized, he said he'd been in such a hurry to get to the hospital that he forgot to mention it and after that got so consumed with his new child that it completely slipped his mind."

"Dad," Billy interrupted. "You have green eyes, I have green eyes, and our name is Cooper. Alex and his ancestors had green eyes, and his sister married a man named William Cooper. My name is William Cooper. Aren't we related to Alex Butler?"

"Oh my, Billy. No, we are not related to Alex, and even if we were, it wouldn't upset me. I'd be happy about it."

Billy whispered, "You really didn't kill the mayor?"

His father shook his head and put his arm around him. "Son, do you remember who you were named for?"

"My great-great grandfather?"

"That's right. When he and his family emigrated in the early 20th century to this country from the Netherlands, they changed their name from DeKuyper to Cooper, and my grandfather's name from Willem to William. By the way, green eyes are common there."

He looked at his son. "That revolver you took, it's more than 100 years old. It belonged to William when he was a sheriff in Ohio."

Billy slumped down on a chair and started to cry. "I've blown it; haven't I? I'm so sorry. All the trouble I got into, it was because I was mad and afraid, and I didn't know what to do."

Greg walked over to his son and put his arms around him. "I understand, and I'm sorry you've been carrying this around for so long. It's a terrible misunderstanding; it's mainly my fault."

He looked at Carrie and Ed. "If I had told my family I was going to see a cardiologist that morning and been forthcoming with you when you interviewed my friends and me, none of this would have happened."

Carrie would call Greg's doctor and Doug Kilmer to verify the story, but she believed him. Relieved that Billy was unharmed and that Greg Cooper, Alex's lifelong friend, was not his killer, they retreated, leaving the family to come to terms with what had happened. Now they were back to square one. Whomever had killed Alex Butler was still out there.

Chapter 56

Ed went home, made himself a cup of tea and entered his study where he sat in a wing chair by a window and thought about the case. Something was missing.

At the start of the investigation, he and Brad had interviewed the mayor's staff and members of the various municipal boards, to assess their culpability as suspects and ascertain whether they had heard or seen anything that would provide information to lead the investigators to find his killer.

They had also spoken with administrators at the school district to see if when he was superintendent, Alex had made enemies there. They struck out. Neither Alex's sister and her family, nor Cheryl's family had anything to add, nor had any other people they had questioned as to possible suspects.

No matter which way they turned, they were repeatedly hitting roadblocks. The person responsible for Alex Butler's death was lurking in the shadows, but who? If he stopped thinking about it, Ed reasoned, maybe something would come to him.

"How about if we drive down to Glenellen Winery on Saturday," Ed suggested a couple of hours later as he and Annie sat at the kitchen table having dinner. "A jazz quartet will be performing that afternoon, starting at 12:30. If we arrive about 11:45, we could have lunch and then spend the afternoon listening to music."

"That sounds lovely, Ed. I'll call Sandy and see if she can come and let Gretchen out around 2:00." She retrieved her cell phone from the counter next to the stove.

A few minutes later, she announced, "She can do it. I'm really looking forward to this."

Chapter 57

Saturday was a cold, bright day, and as Ed and Annie drove down the eastern side of Seneca Lake, snow glistened between rows of buzz-cut corn stalks and sparkled like crystallized sugar on the smattering of grapes that had remained on the vines after the harvest.

The winery was located on a hill with sweeping lake views, and when they entered, a hostess greeted them, gave them each a menu and escorted them to a table. She informed them that they were short-staffed that day and asked that they order their food from the counter in the tasting room and a server would bring their meals to them.

On their way into the restaurant, Annie grabbed some tourist brochures and copies of a weekly newspaper that had been placed on a rack next to the doorway. They were seated at a small table by a window within view of both the lake and the stage where the musicians would be performing.

"Any idea what you want to eat?" Ed asked Annie.

Annie looked at the menu. "I'll have a cup of the butternut squash bisque and a turkey club. What are you having?"

"Guess."

"Hmm. Well, I think you're going to have the tomato bisque, a burger with frizzled onions on a brioche roll, and the sweet potato waffle fries. Am I close?"

Ed laughed. "Right on the money. You know me so well. What would you like to drink?"

"Water and a glass of dry Riesling, please. What are you going to have?"

"Water, and a glass of Cabernet Franc. It should go well with my sandwich."

While she was waiting for Ed to come back from ordering their lunches, Annie picked up the local weekly and started browsing through it, then realized that it was an old edition, dated back to late November. The restaurant obviously hadn't cleared the brochure racks since then. Still, it was something to read until he returned. On the last page was a photo of two men standing beside an eight-point buck with shotguns raised. Annie gasped.

"I ordered a tapenade platter as an appetizer." Ed sat down across from Annie a few minutes later. "They'll bring that with our beverages. I asked that they hold off a while before bringing our soup and sandwiches." Seeing a strange look on her face, he asked, "What's wrong?"

Chapter 58

Annie held the newspaper page up to him with the photo of the two deer hunters. They were dressed in camo jackets and pants, black boots, and knitted skull caps. She pointed to one of them.

"I recognize his name. Josh Ward is the realtor Eve mentioned at our Christmas Eve party, the one who listed their new house. I thought his name seemed familiar, and I just remembered that he was at the museum the Saturday before Alex was killed. I was working in my office and heard the door open, and several people walked in to take a tour of the exhibit.

"I heard him introduce himself to Todd Headley, the docent who was working that day. Later that afternoon, Todd reported that Josh had asked a lot of personal questions about Alex and asked for a business card. He'd read about the field trip to Freedom Hill and said he wanted to contact him to see if he could tag along.

"What if he's the one who asked to be taken off the list of those people Alex discovered were related to his Macyville ancestors? We don't know him, but it's possible he didn't trust Alex and found a way of luring him to Freedom Hill to kill him before Eric and the students arrived."

"Maybe he was just interested in learning more about his heritage."

"Perhaps, but his last name, Ward, is the same as Abraham Butler and Betsey Cooper's half-brother, Hiram, who after the end of the Civil War relocated to Ithaca. Josh Ward probably lives near us, but the article says his brother lives in Watkins Glen, which is only about 20 miles from there.

"As you can see, this paper is printed in black-and-white but look at the headline: *Green with Envy*. I'll read the first two sentences to you: *Folks who know green-*

eyed brothers Joe and Josh Ward are themselves green with envy after learning that the men bagged an eight-point buck on a recent hunting trip. Joe, who lives in Watkins Glen, said he was pleased with how easy it was this year to catch their prey.

"The article says that each of the brothers was carrying a Remington 370 12-gauge shotgun, but they believed that it was the slugs from Joe's gun that felled the animal.

"Ed, you do know that green eyes are a genetic trait that have been passed along through generations of Alex's family."

"Or the fact that they have green eyes could be completely coincidental, Annie."

"But what if it's not, and Josh is Alex's killer? What do you have to lose by interviewing him, even if it's to rule him out?"

"Annie, I'll say something to Carrie about it, but I think I'll let it go for the afternoon and wait until tomorrow. She's so frazzled, that a day without having to deal with police business will be good for her, and even if he is our killer, waiting one more day to interview him won't make a difference."

Chapter 59

Ed called Carrie the next morning at 8:30. "I'm sorry to interrupt your Sunday, Carrie, but I have news to share and didn't think you'd want me to wait until tomorrow to tell you."

"That's okay, Ed. I'm assuming this has something to do with Alex's murder?"

"It does. We have another lead; I'd rather show you than tell you. Can you meet me at your office?"

"How about ten o'clock? We'd planned to take the kids to a movie this afternoon; I want to be home in time for that."

On his way to the meeting, Ed stopped at The Bistro for to-go cups of coffee and freshly baked pumpkin muffins. Sitting with Carrie at a small round table in a corner of her office a few minutes later, Ed pulled the newspaper clipping from his pocket and pointed to the photo of the two men with the deer.

"Annie said Josh visited the museum a few days before Alex was killed and was asking a lot of questions about him. At our Christmas Eve party, we learned from our friends, the Beauvoirs, that he's a realtor and that he recently listed the house they bought in the village. He works for Cove Realty."

He reminded Carrie that Cheryl had said that Alex had contacted someone who wouldn't acknowledge his heritage and demanded that he not contact him again.

"Perhaps the man was Josh Ward. He claimed he was going to call Alex to see if he could tag along on the field trip with Eric and his students, but it's possible he convinced Alex to meet him before the class arrived, maybe indicating that the timing didn't work because of a scheduling conflict.

"When he requested it, Todd Headley, the docent who was working at the museum that day, gave Josh Alex's business card with his cell phone number on it, which might explain why he took his phone. There may have been a log of calls between them.

"There also might have been emails in Alex's laptop, along with the list of the descendants. Josh might not have trusted that his name was deleted from that list. To our knowledge, the only thing on the USB drive was Alex's last audio description, but Josh wouldn't have known that and probably took it, too."

Carrie held her finger up. "Let me do a quick check to get an address for him. If he's working for Cove, I expect he lives close by."

Several minutes later, while Ed sipped coffee and ate his muffin, Carrie looked up.

"There's a realtor named Joshua Ward who resides with his wife, Ellen, at 2311 Sycamore Road on the other side of Silver Bay. They have one daughter. I pulled up a photo from his driver's license. It's the same man as the one in the newspaper article. I'm going to call Brad. I hate to ask him to come in today; I know he and Felicia had planned to go house hunting; if a judge will grant a search warrant, three of us will be better than two."

A couple minutes later, Carrie said, "Brad's on his way. Felicia, apparently, understands and is not upset. He's marrying a good woman."

Ed smiled. "Now, let's go get that search warrant."

Chapter 60

Carrie called a judge and after apologizing for bothering him at home, persuaded him to issue a warrant, explaining that there was a greater probability of finding their suspect at home on a Sunday morning than during the week. Within a couple hours, the three investigators, riding in Brad's unmarked car, headed to the Ward residence.

Snow had fallen overnight, but the roads had been cleared, and it was a bright, sunny day. Instead of taking the highway, Brad decided to drive along the south side of the bay, a scenic route that wound through hundreds of acres of apple orchards and dairy farms with cheese stands.

At the end of the road, he crossed over a small bridge and turned left onto Sycamore Road. The homes were a mixture of styles and sizes, ranging from simple waterfront vacation cottages to permanent year-round dwellings. The Ward family lived in a Craftsman-style bungalow with brown cedar siding, ivory trim and dark green shutters and door.

A flagstone walkway, bisecting the yard, ended at three steps leading up to a covered landing and the front door, which was flanked by wide, mullioned picture windows on either side. Mature rhododendron, azaleas, and holly bushes, neatly trimmed for winter, clustered in groups along the front of the house.

Ed rang the bell, and a slim man of average height, with chiseled features, a trendy five o'clock shadow, dark brown hair clipped short, and clear green eyes opened the door with a small, white, fluffy dog at his side. The dog yipped at the visitors.

"Mollie, quiet," the man admonished the dog. "She won't hurt you; she adores people. Can I help you?" he asked pleasantly.

He was wearing a neat pair of jeans, a horizontal-striped black and forest green crewneck sweater and black loafers.

Carrie handed him the warrant. He said, "I don't understand. What's this about?"

She explained that they were there to interview him, and the warrant gave them permission to search his house; he was a person of interest in Alex Butler's murder. Someone had overheard him asking personal questions about the deceased man at the museum the weekend before he was killed.

"This is a big mistake. I can assure you I had nothing to do with the mayor's death. I have an alibi for the day he was killed. Please come inside so I can straighten this out."

Carrie said, "Ed, I think you and Brad should start searching the premises while I speak with Mr. Ward."

"You don't need to do that, please let me explain."

Ed ignored the man and turned to Brad. "Let's start in the garage and work our way back into the house."

Mollie wandered off, and Ward and Carrie had just sat down in the living room—a long, narrow room with back windows facing a deck and boathouse on the water—when a woman entered.

"Hi, honey, I'm back. I had a good walk. The sun, despite the cold weather, is warm, and the roads are only a bit slushy."

She hesitated when she saw the police chief. A few inches shorter than her husband, she was slender with dark, chin-length straight hair and blue eyes. Ward introduced her.

"This is my wife, Ellen."

Ellen paled when Carrie explained why she was there.

"My husband is not a murderer; you are so wrong," she said and sat on a chair next to her husband.

Carrie considered asking Ellen to leave the room but changed her mind. She wanted to observe her reaction when Josh answered her questions. She explained that someone had recognized Josh and his brother from a newspaper photo—they were standing by a deer they'd killed, both holding Remington 370 12-gauge shotguns, the same make and model that had killed the mayor.

Ward hesitated for a moment, then responded, "I don't own a gun. The one I was using belongs to my brother. When we were hunting and got that buck, the slugs from his rifle killed the deer.

"What I've never told my brother and wouldn't admit to most people, is that I never even tried to hit it, I shot off into the nearby woods. I don't really like to hunt and only do so to bond with Joe. At some point, I'm going to have to break the news to him that I'd rather be hiking in the woods than stalking and killing deer. I did not kill the mayor."

He started walking toward a desk in the corner of the room. Carrie stood up and reached for her gun.

"There's no need for that. I'm not planning to do anything to harm you. There's something in the desk I want to show you."

Ward pulled a card out of a drawer and handed it to Carrie. "Here, take this." It had Chris Bayley's name and phone number on it on it.

"Call Chris; he'll verify I was with him the morning Alex was killed."

Carrie, puzzled, pulled a cell phone out of her pocket, and called the FBI agent, who verified that Josh had been with him the morning of the murder.

She ended the call, turned to Ward, and said, "You're in the clear. Chris says you're a retired FBI agent who occasionally works undercover for the Bureau.

"When we interviewed Chris a second time, it was because we believed he was withholding information about Alex's death that he couldn't share with his friends, but he denied it and said his preoccupation during the first interview was because of another case he was working on. Are you working with him?"

"I am. We're close to solving it, but unfortunately, I can't share the details with you."

"So, the reason for your being at the museum the Saturday before Alex was murdered was truly to view the exhibit?"

"Yes." He explained he was a history buff, had read about the exhibit and decided to spend a little time at the museum that morning. When the tour ended, he asked questions about Alex and his project because of the audio portion of the exhibit that identified Hiram Ward as a half-brother to Abraham Butler and Betsey Cooper. His great-grandfather had the same name and he wondered if they were related.

The docent gave him one of Alex's business cards, and after that, he left because Ellen was lunching with friends, and he needed to pick her up after she finished so they could drive into the city for a visit with their daughter and son-in-law. He planned to call Alex the following week; when he learned he'd been killed, he joined *FindYourRoots.com*.

"I was excited when I signed up, but as it turned out, I'm not related to any of the Macyville settlers. My parents said my Ward ancestors came to this country in the late 1800s from Ireland and Germany. I just wanted to check to make sure they weren't missing something."

Facing the couple, Carrie said, "Apparently, we were on the wrong track; we obviously don't need to be looking for a murder weapon here. I'll call Ed and tell him and Brad to stop the search so we can leave you to the rest of your Sunday."

She dialed Ed's number; when he didn't answer, Cooper said that cell phone service was spotty in their garage.

"If he and Detective Washington aren't back in a few minutes, I'll go get them," Carrie responded.

To pass the time, Carrie and the Wards made small talk, and Carrie noticed a photo on the fireplace mantel of an attractive young couple. She assumed the woman was their daughter; she had the green eyes of her father and the dark hair of her mother, although it was curly, not straight like Ellen's.

"That's our daughter, Kayla," Ellen volunteered. "The man next to her is her husband, Andy."

"Kayla has a degree in communications from Hobart and William Smith and is the director of the Rochester Chamber of Commerce leadership program. She's also taking night classes at St. John Fisher for an MBA. Andy is an accountant with a large firm in the city," she volunteered.

Carrie responded, "She's beautiful and favors both of you."

The couple looked at each other and smiled.

"She looks familiar. I think I've seen her before."

"The Rochester newspaper publishes the Chamber's annual report as an insert in the Sunday paper each year," Ellen replied. "Staff photos have been in the paper many times."

"That might be it," Carrie replied. "I'm going to see where Ed and Brad are. Excuse me for a minute"

Just as she started to leave the room, Ed and Brad approached, carrying a Remington 370 12-gauge shotgun.

Chapter 61

Ed held it up. "Look what we found."

Ward said, "Kayla bought that for my brother. She doesn't hunt, but she knows how passionate he is about it. When she and Andy visited him and his wife in mid-October, he mentioned that his favorite shotgun had seen better days, and he was thinking about buying a new one for hunting season.

"Our daughter and her uncle have always been close, and she decided to surprise him by buying him one for his birthday, which was a week before hunting season started. She stored it in a closet in our basement because she and Andy don't have a secure place to keep it in their condo in the city. During a phone conversation a couple weeks later, he told her he'd decided he didn't want to replace it; it worked fine and fit like a comfortable old shoe.

"She had kept the receipt and called the gun shop to see if she could return it. I remember being surprised that the gun store would take it back. She said it wasn't against the law since it had never been fired. I thought she'd returned it weeks ago.

"That closet is always locked. How did you get into it?"

Ed responded, "We found the gun in the garage, sir. There's a trapdoor with a ladder in the ceiling, weren't you aware of that?"

"We never use it," Ward responded. "When we moved into the house, we cleaned it out; there were old newspapers and pieces of plywood and an old cooler. We have plenty of storage space in the house. We forgot about it. I don't understand why you found our daughter's gun there."

Ed remembered something and asked, "Does Kayla have the same last name as you?"

"No, she's a bit old-fashioned and took her husband's last name, Howard, when they married. Why?"

Ed passed the gun to Brad and looked at Carrie. "Can I speak with you privately for a few minutes?"

A breezeway connected the freestanding garage to the house. Ed motioned to it. "Let's talk there while Brad stays here with the Wards."

Carrie knew better than to question Ed and followed him.

"What's up, Ed?"

"When I did a search for people who had recently purchased guns in our area, Kayla's name came up. I called her; she said she had returned the gun shortly after she purchased it and that she was at the Chamber of Commerce the entire day of Alex's death. When I called the Chamber president, she verified Kayla's alibi.

"What I don't understand is why Kayla would have lied to her parents about returning the gun, and if it's our murder weapon, how she got away with killing him when she had that alibi."

The tiny bud of an idea floating around in Carrie's brain bloomed, and she had an aha! moment. "Ed, did you see the photo of Kayla with her parents in the living room?"

He shook his head.

"Remember, I haven't met Jill Spencer; you and Brad interviewed her, but when I did the background check her driver's license photo came up. She and Ellen could pass as sisters, and except for the curly hair, Kayla looks just like Jill."

"I thought Jill was an only child," Ed responded, "Now that I'm thinking about, when I spoke with Cheryl, she said that Jill's father doted on her. She didn't mention if there were other siblings; I guess I just assumed it."

"In that case, Kayla would be Jill's niece."

Brad appeared and interrupted them. "You need to come back into the living room. Mrs. Ward wants to speak with you."

Chapter 62

Sobbing quietly, Ellen said, "Kayla didn't kill the mayor, and she did plan to return the gun. She's so busy with her job and schoolwork that I offered to return it for her."

The three investigators glanced at each other, not sure where this was going. Ed was the first to speak. "You look remarkably like a woman named Jill Spencer. Are you and she sisters?"

"We're not sisters, but Kayla *is* Jill's child. We adopted her a few days after she was born. She doesn't know; we never told her. I was the one who planned on killing Alex Butler, but I couldn't go through with it."

She explained. She had obtained a bachelor's degree in nursing at Syracuse University, then after she and Josh got married and he obtained work at the FBI field office in Buffalo, she decided to get a master's degree and enrolled at SUNY Buffalo.

One of her classmates was a woman named Jaycee Clark; they looked so much alike that people often mistook them for sisters. She noticed, after a few months, that Jaycee was visibly pregnant. One day they were doing rounds at a local hospital and Ellen congratulated her, but was surprised by her negative reaction.

Jaycee told her that the baby was the result of a relationship that had ended badly, and she had no intention of letting the father know about the pregnancy. He'd caused her horrible emotional distress; he'd been sent a protection from abuse order, and she left him. She said she feared that if she had the child and he learned about it, that he would come after her and the child and they would both be in danger. Reluctantly, to protect her child, she'd decided to put the baby up for adoption.

"I was in a terrible car accident when I was a teenager and as a result was not able to have children. Josh and I agreed when we got married that at some point we would adopt."

She explained that she spoke with Josh, and they concurred that she should ask Jaycee if she were interested in a private adoption. She was, with one condition. The Wards were to never let the child know they were not her birth parents.

The Wards feared it might be difficult to keep that information from her as she got older, but they were desperate for a child and accepted Jaycee's terms. A law in New York state allowed adoptive parents to petition the courts to list their names on the birth certificate, and after they adopted Kayla, they were able to change it.

A few months ago, Kayla told them that she, Andy, and some of their friends had sent DNA samples to *FindYourRoots.com*, just for kicks. Ellen and Josh panicked. What if Kayla learned she had relatives that weren't part of their family? What if she learned about Jaycee or her biological father?

Results came back indicating that she had West African in addition to Scottish and British ancestry. Kayla embraced the results; she figured that since migration patterns started there, it wasn't surprising. After several months passed and no one had been identified as a relative, they started to relax.

A retreat in the Adirondacks for directors of chamber of commerce leadership programs in upstate New York had been scheduled for a weekend late in October. Kayla spent Thursday night with her parents because it would save her an hour's travel time the next day. The attendees were allowed to bring their phones; there was no internet service at the retreat center, computers were to be left at home.

Kayla's husband was away on business. She brought her laptop to her parents' house; she was expecting a grade for a paper she'd written for one of her graduate classes. She gave her mother a list of passwords and asked that she check her emails and text her if the grade came in.

The next day, Ellen opened the laptop and signed into Kayla's email account. There was no grade, but there was an email from *FindYourRoots.com*. Curious, but ashamed she was prying, she opened it. It indicated that there was a 100% match to a male biological parent. To obtain the person's name she needed a password, and after that could click on a link to contact him. She found the password, clicked the link, and followed the prompts. Checking back an hour later, she saw that a man had responded—it was Alex Butler, the mayor.

Ellen was shocked. He was a pillar of the community, and when Kayla was in school, parents and teachers adored him. When he decided to change careers and run for mayor of Lighthouse Cove, everyone she knew was pleased he'd won but sorry he was leaving the school district.

This couldn't be the evil and abusive man Jaycee had told her about. After thinking about it a while, she realized that people could appear one way to the public and be different in their personal lives; it happened all the time.

Deleting the emails, she also canceled the subscription to the ancestry site. Now that he knew Kayla's name, he'd be able to find her. Ellen decided there was no way her daughter was ever going to meet this horrid man. She had to figure out what to do and act quickly. She never said a word about what she'd discovered to Josh.

A few days later, after returning from the conference, Kayla mentioned that she'd not had any notices from *FindYourRoots.com* about possible matches. She knew her grandparents, aunts, uncles, and cousins, but the family was small. Ellen had responded that perhaps there were no other living relatives who had subscribed to the ancestry site. Kayla had submitted her own DNA on a whim and agreed that was possible. She decided to move on.

Chapter 63

A charge nurse at Highland General Hospital in Rochester, Ellen stopped at the grocery store on her way home from work a few days later. A cart bumped into her as she was bending down to pick up a can of pumpkin on a lower shelf. The woman steering the cart apologized; she looked up and recognized Jaycee Clark.

When Ellen called her by name, Jaycee pretended she didn't know her and insisted they'd never met. Ellen persisted, indicating that she wanted to speak with her about something important pertaining to their daughter, and then she admitted who she was.

Jaycee said that she'd gone back to using her birth name, Jill, and had taken the last name of her current husband. They ordered coffee and sat at a table in the supermarket's café and talked.

Ellen explained that through a subscription to *FindYourRoots.com* she'd learned that Alex Butler was Kayla's father, but she canceled the subscription before her daughter could find out about it. She was shocked that a man so many people admired was such an evil person. He hid it well.

Jill seemed horrified and responded that Ellen must find a way to stop Alex from contacting Kayla; he was dangerous, and she had both emotional and physical scars to prove it. She had read in the news about his work on the Macyville project and correctly surmised his reason for joining the ancestry site. It was a fluke that both he and Kayla had registered for it.

Alex could do a lot of psychological damage to Kayla, Jill warned. He would try to manipulate her to hate her parents for not telling her about the adoption and say terrible things about her. She said she'd heard rumors that he was abusive to his current wife and children.

Appalled, Ellen decided that to protect Kayla she would confront Alex and called him the next morning, explaining who she was and how she had learned that he was Kayla's father. She said she and her husband had never told their daughter about the adoption, and she had no idea what to do about it.

He acknowledged he had received the same notification from the ancestry site and was trying to figure out how to handle it, too. He seemed pleasant and eager to speak with her and suggested they meet somewhere private to discuss the situation. He hadn't yet told his wife about Kayla.

Ellen had read about the field trip to Freedom Hill and suggested they meet there an hour before he was to meet the professor and his students. Alex agreed and said he knew the perfect spot, about halfway down the hill at a bench that had been placed next to an historic marker.

"I learned about Alex right around the time Kayla decided to return the gun. After my conversation with Jill, I offered to return it for her. She'd paid by check; I paid her back out of my own account and kept it. I had never even held a shotgun; I took a couple of shooting lessons at the gun club. I'm horrified to admit that I thought about killing him."

Alex had seemed friendly and kind over the phone, and she was starting to have doubts about Jill's story, something about her tale didn't seem authentic, but she decided she had to meet with him anyway. She called Jill and told her what she planned to do.

On the day of the murder, she took a vacation day and drove to Freedom Hill. She had placed the gun in the trunk of her car, intending to use it if she determined Alex was as terrible as Jill had said. Then, horrified, she realized she could never take another life and hid the gun in the garage attic until she could figure out what to do with it.

Alex was sitting on the bench waiting for her. Ellen explained the circumstances of the adoption to him, and in a short time she realized he was not the ogre Jill claimed, but a kind man who until recently had no idea he'd fathered a child with his ex-wife.

He said that he would love to meet Kayla, hoping they could forge some sort of relationship but was also realistic that because of conditions placed on her adoption it might not happen. Although disappointed, he was pleased she was in a stable and loving home and had turned out to be a healthy and productive woman. He would always be available if at some point Ellen and Josh changed their minds and decided to tell her about him. He said he would keep the information confidential except for his wife; he planned on telling her that night.

On her way home, Ellen decided to talk with Josh about Alex, then had second thoughts. It was probably for the best for everyone to pretend the meeting with him had never happened.

Carrie was furious. She looked at Ellen and said, "As you correctly surmised, Alex was a decent and good man, he didn't have an abusive bone in his body, and without going into detail, Jill lied to you about the circumstances of why they divorced. She is a vindictive and nasty person. At least you had the sense, at the last minute, to not do her dirty work for her."

Chapter 64

Josh, appalled, exclaimed, "Why would you keep this from me?"

"I believed Jill at first and panicked. All I wanted to do was protect Kayla," she cried. "I can't believe I even considered killing him. Since I'd shot it, I couldn't return the gun. I hid it in the garage attic because I knew you wouldn't find it and decided that in the spring, I'd take it out in the pontoon and throw it in the bay."

Ed asked, "Did you see anyone else at the site the morning you met with Alex?"

Ellen thought for a minute. "Yes. When I was leaving, I noticed a blue Ford Bronco parked in a driveway next to an old fishing cottage across from the parking lot. I didn't see anyone in it, the windows were tinted. As I drove away, the car entered the lot."

Ed and Brad looked at each other. The car was the same that Jill Spencer drove.

"You're in the clear for now," Carrie said to Ellen. "But you have no alibi, the gun is the same make and model as the one that killed Alex Butler, and it's been shot. We're going to hold on to it just in case you're lying, and by the way, I'd advise you not to leave town," Carrie wrote a receipt and handed it to the distraught woman.

On their way back to the police station, Carrie apprised the men of what she'd learned from Josh and that he was working undercover for the FBI.

"Carrie, the car Ellen described is like the one Jill Spencer drives."

"It's possible it was the same make and model as Jill's, but it couldn't have been hers. Remember, her alibi checked out."

Ed said, "That's true and I believe Jane Thomas when she verified Jill's whereabouts that morning; still, it's possible that she saw only what she wanted to see."

"What do you mean, Ed?" Carrie asked.

"Suppose Annie told me she was taking a day off from work to bake Christmas cookies. I left the house for several hours and when I returned, the cookies were baked, and she was cleaning up the kitchen. I'd probably assume she'd been baking the entire time."

"I see where you're going with this, Ed," Carrie said. "If, while you were gone, Annie realized she was out of some of the ingredients she needed, she might have driven to the grocery store to purchase them and then decided while she was out to run some other errands. She could have been gone an hour or more, and unless she told you about it, you wouldn't have known she hadn't been home all day."

"Exactly. What if Jill's supervisor assumed she was at the hospital all morning, but Jill slipped out and she didn't know about it."

"Wouldn't someone else have noticed?" Brad asked.

"Maybe or maybe not. From Cheryl's account, Jill was quite manipulative when she was younger. We have no idea what really happened that morning."

"I'll schedule another interview with Jane." Ed paused. "Brad, you're not the only one who didn't ask the right questions. I've been an investigator for a long time and should have thought to dig a little deeper when I interviewed her the first time. I must be slipping."

"Ed, there's no reason to beat yourself up about it. Remember, the Spencers had alibis, and we didn't find any guns in the house when we searched it," Brad said, then thought for a few seconds. "What if Jill borrowed one?"

Recalling that Jill had said her father had died recently and that she had hunted with him, Ed replied, "We're on the same track, Brad. If her mother is still living in the house where Jill was raised, it's possible she hasn't yet given away her husband's possessions, including his gun collection. Perhaps Jill took one of them, killed Alex and returned it without her mother realizing it was gone."

Carrie said, "I want to spend some time with my family; I expect the two of you have other things to do on this fine Sunday morning. I'll check tomorrow morning to see if Jill's mother still lives in the area.

"If she does, I'll call and schedule an interview and then contact a judge to execute a search warrant in case she's not cooperative. Let's keep in touch and meet here tomorrow around 2:00."

"Carrie, in the meantime, what can I do to help?" Brad asked.

"Go spend the rest of the day with Felicia. If Jill's mother is still living in that house and I can obtain a warrant, I'd like you to accompany me when I interview her. Maybe by tomorrow we will have finally closed this case."

Chapter 65

At 8:00 the next morning, after pouring herself a cup of coffee from the pot in the lobby, Carrie opened her computer to the local white pages and within minutes discovered that Joan Clark still lived in the house where she and her husband had raised Jill. She obtained a search warrant and called the woman, who hesitated at first, then agreed to speak with her. The call ended and Brad strolled in.

"Hi, Brad, what's up?"

"Scott Peterson's in the lobby. He says he wants to speak with you about the murder investigation."

"Bring him in." In less than a minute, Brad returned with the visitor.

Peterson owned a 300-acre apple farm just outside the village. A stocky man of medium height with a ruddy complexion, close-cropped grey hair, and blue eyes with laugh lines at the corners, he wore jeans, a plaid shirt, a blue blazer, and brown loafers.

The press release Carrie had sent out early in January had generated no leads. As a last-ditch attempt, Carrie had sent another to all media outlets the previous Friday, hoping, yet again, to jog someone's memory who might have seen or heard something that would help them solve the case. Peterson had read the article in the Sunday paper.

"Let's go and sit at the table; it'll be more comfortable," Carrie suggested, walking over to the small round table placed in one corner of her office. He refused her offer of a beverage and began to talk.

He said the day of Alex's murder, he and his wife, Julia, were preparing for a trip to their vacation home in the southwest mountains of Virginia to celebrate Thanksgiving with their family. They planned to stay there and not return to Lighthouse Cove until just before Christmas.

His wife had assembled a basket of apple products including pie filling, cider, jelly, and streusel muffins that she wanted to give to her friend, a neighbor who lived with her husband two doors away, for Thanksgiving. She asked Scott to walk the gift down to their house while she finished packing.

"I had no idea that the mayor was meeting with the college students and their professor at Freedom Hill that day, so what I observed at the time had no significance. Now, it does.

"There's a small fishing cottage between our house and our neighbors. The owners rent it out in the spring and summer; it's vacant the rest of the year. I noticed a blue Ford Bronco parked in the driveway."

Carrie glanced at Brad. That was the same car Ellen Ward had claimed to see the day Alex was killed.

"The motor was running, I thought perhaps the driver had pulled in to make a phone call and have a smoke."

"A smoke?" Carrie asked.

"Yes, the window on the driver's side was cracked open and I could smell cigarette smoke."

"Could you see the person who was in the car?"

He shook his head. "The back and side windows were tinted. I did notice the license plate; it was clever, ESRUN1#, especially when I noticed a hospital parking sticker on the bumper."

"#1NURSE, spelled backward." Brad said. "Carrie, can you guess whose plate that is?"

Carrie nodded. "Yes, we can talk about it after Mr. Peterson is finished here. Mr. Peterson, please continue."

"I didn't think much about it, delivered the basket, and when I was walking back to our house, I noticed the car was now parked in the Freedom Hill parking lot. A woman got out, opened the back door, took out a hunting jacket and a pair of hunting pants and after she put those on, tucked her long, dark hair into a cap, opened her trunk and pulled out a shotgun.

"I wondered if she'd parked there to meet someone to go hunting in the woods east of Freedom Hill, since there's no hunting allowed at the historic site."

"Did you see what she was wearing before she put the hunting gear on?"

"It looked like she was wearing some sort of uniform, dark red or burgundy, like nurses' scrubs, which would make sense given her license plate."

"Did you hear any shots?"

"Not at first, but several minutes later, I heard three as I was walking down the driveway to our house. At the time, I figured they were from hunters' guns."

Scott continued. He and his wife drove to Virginia, not knowing about the mayor's murder. Their home was in a remote part of Virginia, and they were unplugged.

"Our cell phones don't work there; we have a landline, and if we want to use internet, we need to go to the café at the supermarket in the nearby town. We have a TV antenna, no cable, so we get only a few local channels. We had no idea the mayor had been killed."

He and his wife returned to Lighthouse Cove a week before Christmas. He'd made plans to meet some friends for breakfast at Vic's Diner a few days later and arrived earlier than the rest of the group. While he was waiting, he picked up the daily paper from the counter and read an article announcing that the village had received a state grant for a beach reclamation project. The reporter had interviewed the mayor, Janice Shaheen.

"I wondered what had happened to Alex. When my friends arrived, I asked. They said he'd been murdered at Freedom Hill early in November before Thanksgiving. I was shocked, but even then, I didn't connect the dots."

"What changed?"

"The article in this week's Sunday paper mentioned the exact date the mayor was killed. I realized it was the same day I took the apple basket to our friends and saw the car and the woman with the rifle. It may be nothing, still, I felt duty-bound to speak with you about it."

Carrie stood up and shook his hand.

"Thank you for coming in. You may have provided information that will finally help us apprehend our killer. Would you be willing to be a witness at a trial?"

"Of course. My wife and I met Alex and his wife at social functions. They were a delightful couple, and he did a fine job as mayor. If the woman I saw is his killer, she should spend the rest of her life in jail."

Carrie thanked him again. After he left, she looked at Brad. "That plate is Jill Spencer's, isn't it?"

"Yes. I noticed it when Ed and I left the Spencer's house after interviewing them. Remember, I told you she smelled of cigarette smoke but when her husband mentioned it, she said it was because she walked by a group of men who were smoking at Apex. When I searched her car that day, I smelled the smoke, but figured it had lingered from her encounter at the gas station."

"Caught in yet another lie," Carrie said. "Let's go get that warrant."

She called Ed; his phone went to voice message. Within minutes, she and Brad were heading to Jill Spencer's mother's home.

Chapter 66

They parked in the circular driveway of a grand, brick, Georgian house with white pillars and a cupola on the roof. Large, fluffy hydrangeas, now brown and papery, clustered in groups along the front of the house, interspersed with wheat-colored ornamental grasses. Brick steps led to a small porch and a white door. Carrie rapped on a large iron lion's head knocker.

Joan Clark, a trim woman with greying blond hair cut straight to her chin, greeted them. She had blue eyes that matched the color of the cashmere twin set she was wearing, a string of pearls around her neck and small pearl earrings. Grey woolen trousers and charcoal ballet slippers completed the outfit.

"My bridge club is coming for a late lunch today; I'm hoping we can end this interview before then."

The house had a center hall with ornate steps curving up to a second-floor landing. A living room filled with antique furniture, large Impressionist paintings, and a scattering of Oriental rugs was visible to the right of the hall; to the left, a dining room with a crystal chandelier and a massive rectangular mahogany table set with cream-colored linens, simple ivory and gold dishes, gold-rimmed goblets—and from its patina—what appeared to be antique silverware.

"How may I help you?"

Carrie said that they were there because they were investigating Alex Butler's murder and after they learned that he'd once been married to Jill, they interviewed her and her husband. During the interview, Jill had volunteered that while he was alive, she'd hunted with her father.

"She did."

"Would you still happen to have his guns?"

"He died a year ago, and I haven't yet had the physical or emotional energy to go through his things; the guns are locked away in a safe in a closet in our basement."

Carrie handed her the search warrant. "Is it possible that Jill could have borrowed one of your husband's guns during hunting season without your knowing about it?"

"Yes. She hardly ever visits and then only when Dan encourages it, but she's always had a key to the house and has been free to come and go as she pleases. I am a busy woman with my club and volunteer work and am not home much during the day." Then it hit her. "Oh my, do you think Jill killed Alex?"

"Why would you ask?"

"You must know the reason she and Alex married is because Jill claimed she was pregnant. Jill hated Alex and told us terrible stories about the way he treated her after they separated. She claimed she lost the baby because he had physically and emotionally abused her and after that, he kicked her out.

"My husband believed her and wanted to press criminal charges against him, but she never had a physical mark on her body, no visible signs that she was pregnant, and never called the police when the abuse supposedly happened.

"I didn't believe the pregnancy story; it was a ruse to get him to marry her. The accusations she made against him were a vendetta because for once in her life she couldn't talk her way out of a bad situation of her own making.

"I pleaded with my husband to let it go, and then Jill asked him to drop it, saying she just wanted to get on with her life. I realized the real reason was because if Alex were charged with assault the truth would be revealed, and everyone would learn what really happened.

"I had once overheard her speaking on the telephone to a girlfriend after she started dating him. She said she'd get him to marry her whatever the cost.

"In her fashion, Jill loved her father and shortly after she and Alex split up, he had the first of several heart attacks. She finally admitted she'd lied about the pregnancy and Alex's supposed abusive behavior; after that their relationship changed—there wasn't quite the loving glow in my husband's eyes when she entered a room.

"When she left for graduate school later that summer, we didn't see her for more than a year. She said it was because graduate school nurses were expected to work on holidays, and she was busy on weekends. We offered to visit her in Buffalo—it's a short drive—but she kept on putting us off. I guess she was ashamed or embarrassed to be with us, although before then I'd never seen her show any remorse for what she'd done to hurt others. It wasn't in her nature.

"My daughter is emotionally damaged and amoral, and I don't know why. When she was a little girl, she asked for a very expensive doll for Christmas. It was all the rage that year. It's not that we couldn't afford it, but most toy stores were sold out of it, and parents were lining up at 2:30 in the morning to be there when the stores that carried them opened. My husband was willing to stand in line in the middle of the night, but I was not and convinced him that Jill wouldn't be irreparably harmed if we told her she'd eventually get the doll, just not for Christmas.

"She went into her room and destroyed a few of her better dolls in spite. Again, my husband wanted to capitulate, but I told him that if we gave in to her, the bad behavior would continue. He finally agreed with me that her punishment should be based on consequences. Since she couldn't respect what she had, we told her we weren't going to buy her the doll she coveted. We didn't want her to destroy it, too, in a fit of pique. It was hard for my husband, but he realized we were doing the right thing.

"A few days later, she came home from school with the exact doll she'd asked for. She said a classmate had allowed her to borrow it, but that night we got a call from the child's parents. Jill had blackmailed the girl. Even though it wasn't true, she'd threatened to tell their teacher the child had cheated on a math test unless she gave Jill the doll.

"We returned it, of course, and then scheduled some counseling sessions for ourselves and for Jill, we wanted to nip the bad and willful behavior in the bud. It seemed to work; there were no other incidents like that, at least not that we knew of, but she was always a challenge. We were so pleased when she started to date Alex, and then when they married. We expected him to be a good influence on her.

"We tried our best to raise her to have good values, but something in her soul is corrupted. She's had two decent husbands. Alex was a sweet, kind, and lovely man; Dan is, too. I don't believe she's been able to appreciate what she has."

Carrie asked Joan to take her and Brad to the gun safe. She retrieved a key from a drawer in the kitchen, led them down the stairs to a finished basement with a wide screen TV, bookshelves and comfortable chairs and sofas and inserted the key into the lock of the safe. Inside were several rifles—one was a Remington 370 12-gauge. Joan said the Remington was Jill's, her husband had preferred to hunt with a variety of Winchester models—the other rifles in the case.

Donning gloves, Brad and Carrie examined all the rifles. Except for the Remington, they looked as though they'd never been used. Apparently, Jill's father had been meticulous about keeping them clean. The Remington had some carbon inside the barrel, and they were hoping there would be fingerprints on the outside of the gun.

Carrie asked if Mrs. Clark's husband had stored ammunition in the safe. She pointed to a shelf and pulled out two boxes, each indicating that there were 20 shells inside. One was unopened; the other had 17—three were missing.

Brad peered closely into the box. Inside, he found a long, dark hair. Retrieving tweezers from his pocket he held it up for Carrie to see, then placed it in an evidence bag he'd removed from a pocket. "The 'smoking gun'."

Carrie asked, "Would you happen to have anything with Jill's DNA on it? A hairbrush, some items of clothing?"

Joan thought for a minute. "Possibly. Before she married Dan, she visited us during holidays and vacations, and then they visited us together a couple times a year until they moved back to Lighthouse Cove. It was mainly to see her father; she had little time for me because she knew I saw through her and detested how she manipulated him. There should be a hairbrush in one of the dresser drawers in her room. You're welcome to it."

She led them to the room and handed them the brush. Carrie presented the woman with a receipt for that item, the gun, and ammunition box.

As she escorted them to the front door, Joan shook her head and said to Carrie, "Cheryl was one of Jill's closest friends when they were growing up and didn't deserve to lose Alex the way she did. I feel so sad for her and her family, more so if my daughter is the architect of their pain."

She slumped into a chair in the foyer and whispered, "Oh, my, Jill, whatever have you done?"

Back in the car Brad remarked, "It's interesting that Jill never came home for a year or let her parents visit her at grad school after she and Alex split."

"You know why that is. She didn't want them to know she really was pregnant and planned to give the baby up for adoption. Joan will probably learn she has a granddaughter when it comes out in the trial. Poor woman."

Carrie called the forensic office in Williamson to let them know Brad would be dropping off evidence for them to analyze.

"Yes, okay, that makes sense. Thanks." Carrie hung up the phone and turned to Brad.

"They suggested that all the evidence be transferred to the Rochester forensic office; they have the capability of conducting rapid DNA tests there, and we could have the results by mid-afternoon instead of in several days.

"After you drop me off at the station, go to the Williamson forensic office and pick up that evidence that's being stored there. They'll have everything ready for you."

Carrie had just sat down at her desk when Ed called.

"Is the interview room available?"

"It is; why?"

"I just got off the phone with Jane Thomas. She was finishing a meeting with Bonnie Caruso, her administrative assistant, when I called earlier. She put me on speaker phone. After we hung up, she explained to Bonnie what the call had been about, and then called me back. Bonnie blew Jill's alibi out of the water; she lied about her whereabouts the morning Alex was killed.

"Jill's working until 3:30 today, and the nurses' station is just down the hall from Jane's office; we agreed it would be better for them to come to us, so we can talk privately. She and Bonnie will be here shortly."

"I'd like to sit in on this one, Ed. It appears the noose is starting to tighten around Jill Spencer's neck. I'll tell you about it when you get back to the station."

"I'm on my way. I'll see you in a few minutes."

Chapter 67

"Scott Peterson identified the license plate of a car he saw that was parked across the street from the Freedom Hill parking lot the morning Alex was killed," Carrie explained, "and later in the parking lot. It matched Jill's and he said he'd smelled cigarette smoke wafting from the car. When the forensic techs combed the crime scene for evidence, they collected all sorts of trash, including cigarette butts.

"I expect the hair samples from the ammunition box and her hairbrush we retrieved at Joan Clark's house are going to match the hair sample found in Alex's car, along with the fingerprints on the gun and on the box. And I'm willing to bet that Jill's DNA will be on those cigarette butts."

Ed agreed and reminded her when he and Brad questioned Jill and her husband, cigarette smoke permeated her clothing. She claimed it was because men were smoking out front of the gas station when she went to retrieve her receipt; when Carrie called the manager, he couldn't recall that the men had been smoking.

"I am so sorry that I didn't have all the information you needed the first time you interviewed me," Jane said minutes later when she, her assistant, Bonnie, and Carrie and Ed were seated around the table in the interview room.

"I truly believed she'd been in the building all day. She was doing a double shift and after the first one ended, she came to me and said she wasn't feeling well. I asked if she wanted to go home; she replied that she thought she was just tired, and maybe needed some food and asked if she could rest for a while."

If she'd gone home, she wouldn't have had anyone to vouch for her alibi, Carrie thought.

"I had back-to-back meetings that morning and suggested that Jill rest in one of the rooms adjacent to the nurses' breakroom that had been set up for that purpose and said I'd check on her between meetings.

"Jill went into the room, put her purse on a shelf, took off the sweater she'd been wearing over her scrubs, set it on a chair and got into the small cot that had been placed along a wall. I notified the other nurses on the shift that they'd be down one person for a few hours. Fortunately, it was a slow day, and no one had a problem with the others covering for her."

Jane explained that between her first and second meetings, she checked on Jill. It appeared she'd taken a nap, the sheets were mussed, and although her sweater and purse were still there, she wasn't. She asked the nurses on her floor if anyone had seen her. One nurse replied that she'd mentioned going to the cafeteria for something to eat.

"When I returned from my second meeting, Jill was on the floor, joking with some of the residents. She thanked me for being so understanding and said she felt much better. I had no reason to believe she wasn't in the hospital the entire morning."

"I didn't know about any of this," Bonnie said, "until your call this morning, Mr. DeCleryk. When Jane hung up, I asked her why you had questions about Jill Spencer, and she told me what was going on. I was astounded. I saw Jill entering the employee parking lot around 9:00 the morning Alex Butler was murdered.

"I had to leave work right around that time for a family emergency. My son's school had called; he was complaining of severe pain in his stomach and was spiking a fever. I had just gotten into my car, hadn't even turned on the engine, when Jill pulled into the spot next to me. It was between shifts and the daytime workers had started at 8:30, but I didn't think much about it at the time. I figured maybe she was coming in late because she'd had an appointment or something.

"I was concerned about my son, Nathan, and after I picked him up at school, I drove him to his pediatrician who diagnosed him with appendicitis. He was concerned it was about to burst, so I drove him to Children's Hospital, where his appendix was removed within the hour. I'm a single parent and took family leave for several days. I didn't learn about your interview with Jane until now."

Chapter 68

The investigation had been like a huge working ship, picking up bits and pieces of cargo at various ports until reaching the terminus at the end of its journey. The investigators believed they had enough evidence to charge Jill Spencer with the murder of Alex Butler, but for an airtight case decided not to arrest her until they heard back from the forensic office.

The DNA results were confirmed at 3:15, shortly before Jill ended her shift at the hospital, a couple hours after Brad had returned from Rochester. The three investigators drove to the Spencer house to arrest her. She was walking up the driveway when she turned around and saw them getting out of the car and walking toward her.

"You know why we're here?" Ed asked.

For a split second her eyes hardened, then she broke into a big smile. "Did the men I saw at the gas station kill Alex? Did I help you solve the case?" she asked brightly

Carrie said, "No, you know that was your attempt to get us off track with our investigation. We're here to arrest you for the murder of Alex Butler," Carrie Mirandized and handcuffed her.

"I want to call my husband," she responded. "Then I want to call my attorney."

They charged her with first degree murder and Carrie escorted Jill to an interview room where she placed two calls. Within minutes, her husband and attorney arrived.

Paula Fagan had dark brown eyes, brown hair cut in a geometric bob, and was wearing a deep red skirt suit and black stiletto heels. Her only accessories were a diamond eternity wedding band on her left ring finger and small, round diamond stud earrings. She asked the investigators and Dan to leave the room while she conferred with her client, and several minutes later, called them back in.

She cautioned, "You don't need to say anything, Jill."

"That's true, Jill, you don't need to say a thing, but it will go better for you if you cooperate," Carrie countered.

Paula scoffed. "This is a witch hunt for sure. Why would you believe my client murdered Alex Butler? She had an ironclad alibi the morning he was killed; her supervisor confirmed it."

Carrie responded, "About that. As it turns out, there was no alibi plus we have witnesses who saw her at the scene of the crime and entering the parking lot of the hospital after Alex was killed. And then there's that DNA and other evidence tying her to the crime, but as you know, we're not obligated to give you those specifics right now.

"There's no doubt in my mind that Jill will be convicted at her trial, and if there were a death penalty in New York she'd get it."

Jill took a deep breath, rolled her eyes, folded her arms across her chest. "As Paula has instructed me, I'm not saying anything except that I can give you the name of the person who really killed Alex."

Paula, shocked, looked at Jill. "Why am I hearing about this just now?"

"She's grasping at straws," Ed replied. "There was someone she tried to manipulate to do her dirty work for her, but at the last minute, the woman realized that Jill had played her and although she met him the morning he was killed, she never had a gun with her."

Dan, who had been eerily quiet, said," What are you talking about?"

"Yes, what are you talking about?" Paula echoed.

"Do you want to tell them or should I?" Ed asked.

Jill smirked. "Be my guest."

"After Jill and Alex split because she'd faked a pregnancy, she discovered she really was pregnant and months later gave birth to the child, a girl, who she then gave up for adoption. She hated Alex so much that she tried to manipulate one of the adoptive parents to kill him, hoping she wouldn't have to do it herself; it didn't work."

"Honey, I tried to tell him," Jill responded, looking at her husband with pleading eyes. "I called and emailed Alex when I discovered I was pregnant, hoping he'd believe me, and we'd reconcile. He never responded. I sent him a letter, but it came back address unknown, and none of his friends would tell me where he was living. I had no choice but to give up the baby for adoption. I didn't tell you about it because I was afraid you wouldn't want me if you knew," she whined. "That doesn't mean I killed him."

Dan had been listening quietly. "That makes no sense. Of course, I would have wanted you. Why would you even think that?" Then it hit him that she was trying to manipulate him, too.

"You vowed you'd never keep secrets from me, Jill. All I'm hearing is one lie after another, and I'm wondering what else you've lied about over the years. Sadly, I believe the investigators.

"When you told me about faking the pregnancy, you seemed to be truly contrite, but I realize now that you're not the woman I thought you were. I've tried my best to make you happy. We've certainly had our ups and downs; I figured all couples have rough patches that they weather. What you've done is reprehensible."

He threw his hands up as if to ward off an attack, walked toward the door, then turned to his wife, his eyes filled with anger and despair. "I'm going over to my brother's house and explain to him what happened. I'll be living there until I can find my own place. I'll be filing for divorce this week."

"Good riddance," Jill scoffed.

Hours later she was arraigned, denied bail, and remanded to the county jail to await trial.

Chapter 69

A couple hours later, the investigators were toasting their success at The Brewery when Brad said, "I'm curious about something. When we interviewed the Spencers, they presented a united front; they appeared to be happy. How could Jill turn on him so quickly?"

Ed responded, "Their relationship was based on him adoring her and for the most part her getting her way. That changed when she couldn't manipulate him into refusing the job offer with Motts. He started showing some backbone, and I suspect from that point her feelings for him changed. When he didn't defend her when we said she'd murdered Alex, she had no further use for Dan—the classic symptoms of someone with a narcissistic personality disorder."

Ed went home; now that the case was closed, Brad decided to take a few days off, called Felicia and then left to meet with her and a realtor. Carrie walked back to her office. She was exhausted and had just closed her eyes when her phone rang. It was the DA, Sean O'Leary.

"Paula Fagan called me a little while ago. Jill wants to make a deal."

Carrie laughed. "We have her dead to rights, Sean; there's so much evidence no jury will acquit her. What could she possibly offer you?"

"Paula said Jill would waive her right to a trial and plead guilty if we agree that instead of 25 to life, she'd serve 15 to 40 years with eligibility for parole in 15. Usually that sentence is given because there are extenuating circumstances, like a battered wife who finally had enough, but I spoke with a judge, and we're considering it.

"It will save the taxpayers' money, and the Butler and Ward families won't have to endure sitting through a trial and having all the ugly details about why she killed Alex aired in public. Jill doesn't want her mother to learn about Kayla."

"She has no control over that, Sean. If the Wards decide to let Cheryl Butler know that Alex had a daughter, they could decide at the same time to contact Joan Clark."

"I'm not going to be the one to remind her of that, Carrie. Personally, I'd like to get this case off the docket as soon as possible."

"Is she going to be required to give an allocution statement?"

"No. Paula offered one; when I spoke with the judge, we agreed it would be a waste of everyone's time because Jill's shown no remorse."

"I'm uncomfortable with this, Sean. We still have some unanswered questions that will help us tie up the missing pieces on the case."

"How about if we make the deal conditional upon her answering them?"

"That works for me. Brad's taking a few vacation days, but I'd like Ed DeCleryk to be there when I interview her. I'm assuming you'll also want to be present?"

"Yes. I'll call Paula as soon as we hang up, and if Jill agrees, I'll schedule a time for tomorrow and get back to you."

Chapter 70

Sean called Carrie several minutes later. Jill had accepted the terms of the plea deal. Carrie texted Brad with an update, called Ed, then headed home. Although relieved the case was finally solved, she felt sad and depressed, and she was exhausted.

As soon as she entered her house, Matt greeted her with a kiss, and Natalya and Arturo ran over to her and hugged her legs. She smiled, pleased to see her family and grateful for the life she had with a caring husband and two healthy, active children. They had already had their supper. Matt had bathed them, and they were ready for bed.

She read a story to Natalya, then tucked her in and kissed her goodnight while Matt did the same with Arturo. Later, the couple sat at the kitchen table eating chili, while Carrie apprised him of the events leading up to Jill's confession.

Yet again she was torn about what she wanted to do with her job. She felt a sense of satisfaction about solving the case, but she missed her children and was troubled that she had so little energy left to deal with them when she returned home each night.

During the murder case, Matt had taken the lion's share of responsibilities for the house and children and didn't seem to resent it, still, she felt guilty. Maybe a nine-to-five job working for the police academy was the best solution.

She'd been interviewed and offered the job but had stalled giving them an answer. The recruiter explained to her that she wouldn't need start until fall; she could take her time deciding, although they needed to know no later than April so they could continue the search if she refused the offer.

"I don't know what to do, Matt. I desperately want a job that doesn't conflict so much with family time, but even with the challenges, I love what I'm doing."

"Carrie, I have an idea that might work."

He explained. Carrie grinned and hugged her husband. "Brilliant. I don't know why I didn't think of it. Let's get the ball rolling."

Chapter 71

Ed called Josh Ward to let him know they'd arrested Jill Spencer for Alex's murder and gave details of the plea deal. Josh was pleased. Ellen might have been required to testify at a trial and the Butlers would learn all the sordid details about how she contemplated killing Alex herself. He said he'd call Chris Bayley and ask that he inform the rest of Alex's friends.

"There's something else I want to discuss with you," Ed said. They spoke for several minutes, and then he called Cheryl Butler to tell her about Jill's arrest, the plea deal, and about Kayla.

Cheryl cried, appalled that an incident that occurred almost 30 years ago would lead to her husband's murder. "Jill is such a sick, disturbed woman, Ed, I'll never understand that level of hatred. I'm glad there will be no trial. My family and the Wards won't be called as witnesses or be subjected to a long and drawn-out process that will reveal all the terrible and sordid details of why she wanted him dead.

"In some misguided way she may have believed that with her being pregnant, Alex would have reconciled with her for the baby's sake, but he wouldn't have, although he certainly would have paid child support and shared custody. At the time, he thought she was harassing him, which is why he didn't respond to her calls and emails. I wonder if he had called her back if he'd still be alive."

"We'll never know the answer to that, Cheryl, but I doubt it. Jill's desire for revenge started when Alex divorced her and then later when you married him. After she and Dan moved back to Lighthouse Cove, she was constantly reminded of what she'd lost."

"At least now I'm pretty sure I know what Alex wanted to discuss with me when we spoke the night before he was killed. He wanted to tell me about Kayla. Do you think it would be okay for me to contact the Wards?"

"Kayla doesn't know she's adopted; it was a condition of the agreement with Jill. Josh said given Jill's arrest, he thinks it's time for the secrets to end and for Kayla to learn about the circumstances of her birth; he believes Ellen will concur.

"The news may be difficult for her to digest, especially given that her birth mother murdered her biological father. I'd hold off calling. I expect someone from the family will contact you if Kayla decides she's ready to meet you and your children."

Promising to keep in touch, Ed ended the conversation. Gretchen was scratching at the back door, needing to go out; he accompanied her. The sky was clear, brilliant with a thick blanket of stars, the full moon creating a white, luminescent path on the water. Despite the chill in the air, he started a fire in the outdoor fireplace, turned on two, tall patio heaters, retrieved a couple chairs and a small table from the shed, and went back inside for a bottle of red wine and a plate of cheese and crackers.

Annie arrived home minutes later. The couple sat quietly and talked, Ed summarizing the events of the day.

"I'm glad the case is closed, Ed. Still, the entire situation saddens me," Annie said.

"Me, too, Annie. After we meet with Jill tomorrow, we should have all our remaining questions answered. After that's over, I don't plan on taking on any more consulting jobs for the next several months. I desperately need a break."

Chapter 72

The next morning Carrie, Ed and the DA met with Paula Fagan and Jill at the jail.

Ed was surprised at how much she'd aged in 24 hours. Her beautiful, shiny dark hair hadn't been washed, and it was lank and oily. Without makeup, worry lines crisscrossed her face, like streets and alleyways in a dangerous part of town. Her blue eyes, dark circles under them, reminded him of shiny, opaque pebbles strewn askew for unsuspecting passersby to trip on.

The DA said, "If you plead guilty and waive your right to a trial, you'll serve 15 to 40 years and be eligible for parole in 15 years, but as a condition of the deal you will need to be forthcoming about the planning and execution of the murder. Chief Ramos will be questioning you. Your answers will be recorded."

To no one's surprise, hatred, jealousy, resentment, and anger were the four pillars upon which her crime stood. In short, she hated Alex because he caught her in a lie, divorced her and married Cheryl. She admitted she gave Kayla up for adoption because not only did she not want her, but she was also determined that neither Alex nor Cheryl would have a presence in her daughter's life.

She was jealous of Cheryl for having what she felt should have been hers and resented the couple for the life they'd carved out for themselves and their family. She'd harbored anger about it for years, but it lay for years as if in a shallow grave waiting for a flood to wash the dirt away and expose the coffin.

Her rancor had remained below the surface until she and Dan moved back to Lighthouse Cove. There she was constantly reminded of what she'd lost when Alex and Cheryl's names appeared in the paper, and when she read about his work with the historical society and success in getting the grant to rebuild Macyville.

Her opportunity came when she bumped into Ellen Ward at the supermarket. She hoped Ellen would be the weapon that would end Alex, but pragmatic and resourceful, she decided to follow her to Freedom Hill in case Ellen had second thoughts and she'd have to finish the job herself. She believed she'd constructed a perfect alibi and was baffled when it fell apart.

She confirmed that she shot Alex in the knees so he couldn't run away, then shot him in the throat as a symbolic way of silencing him forever. She seemed gleeful when she described the look on Alex's face when he recognized her and realized she was going to kill him.

As they expected, she admitted to taking his cellphone and laptop. She'd placed them in a garbage bag and discarded them in a construction dumpster, not because there was incriminating evidence, but because she wanted the investigators to conclude that his death had been the result of his work with the historical society. She said there was no USB drive; it was one piece of the puzzle that was missing.

The investigators and DA were chilled by her lack of contrition. Carrie shut off the recorder. Jill was escorted back to her jail cell.

On their way out of the building, Ed turned to Carrie. "You supported Sean's decision to allow Jill to plead. I'd say it was a generous deal for a person who committed premeditated, cold-blooded murder and shows no remorse. With all the evidence we had, there's no way she would have been acquitted if there'd been a trial."

"I know. But as we discussed before, the families she harmed won't have to sit through a trial or be called as witnesses, plus it keeps Jill's dirty laundry tucked away in the bin where it belongs. And we were able to tie up loose ends."

Carrie smiled. "As you well know, Ed, there was no promise made to release Jill after 15 years; the parole board will only review her case, and I expect parole will never be granted. Jill's so narcissistic that she's probably incapable of repenting and even if she is a model prisoner, the parole board will pick up on it.

"Paula had no illusions when she encouraged Jill to take the deal. My sense is that she doesn't like to lose, and she quickly ascertained that this case wouldn't be a win for her if it ever went to trial. Now she can brag that she negotiated a sweet deal for her client. She's aware that Jill will most likely spend the rest of her days in prison."

Chapter 73

Cheryl Butler had taken a leave of absence to deal with the aftermath of Alex's death. The following Thursday morning, she decided that while she wasn't quite prepared to give away all of Alex's belongings, she could donate some of his coats and jackets to the Community Closet at Peace Church so that those in need would have something warm to wear during the remaining snowy and rainy months of winter.

She walked into the foyer and opened the closet door. Starting at the back, she pulled out several coats and jackets that had been stored there since last fall. As she sorted through each one, she went through the pockets to make sure they were empty. The last was Alex's rain jacket, and it was there she found not one, but two USB drives.

She remembered that the night before the field trip it had rained. Alex must have placed the drives in the pocket of his jacket, expecting the rain to continue throughout the next day.

By the time he was ready to leave for his first meeting, the rain had stopped, the temperature had plummeted, and she believed at the last minute he replaced the jacket for a warmer one. In his haste to get to his meeting with Ellen Ward, he forgot to remove the drives.

Inserting one of the drives into a USB port on her computer, she discovered the final audio description he'd recorded. To her surprise, the second one contained all the files pertaining to his work on the Macyville project including the list of the descendants of the Butler, Cooper, and Ward clans with names, addresses and phone numbers so Annie could invite them to the grand opening.

She called Annie, and shortly after, got into her car and drove to the museum

Audio #5—Conclusion

From the time it was established in the early 1850s until it was abandoned in the mid-1920s, Macyville had been a shelter in the storm for escaping slaves and a haven for freed people of color. But there were many challenges along the way.

The Fugitive Slave Act of 1850 created obstacles for free states harboring escaped slaves, and until the Emancipation Proclamation was signed by President Lincoln, there were numerous unsuccessful attempts by Federal agents to breech the settlement with the purpose of capturing and returning the fugitives to their masters.

Local businessmen, determined to acquire part of the land for industrial and commercial purposes, tried repeatedly to pressure Macy to sell it; when he refused, they attempted, to no avail, to pressure elected officials to rezone it.

In 1860, Macy added a clause to his will and a covenant to the deed that guaranteed the settlers a home for as long as they wished; the fugitives, a safe haven until they could escape to freedom; and restricted land use to historic preservation or for nature conservation if at some point the settlement was abandoned. An honored, respected, and beloved member of the community, he died in 1890.

Once or twice a decade, puzzling fires erupted that were quickly extinguished and caused little damage. But in 1934, a massive conflagration spread quickly through the abandoned settlement and destroyed most of the remaining buildings. Yet again, fire investigators believed the cause to be arson but were never able to tie anyone to the crimes.

Macy's heirs razed the burnt-out shells of buildings, planted trees, and established a nature preserve with walking trails that led to Freedom Hill and the beach below. The preserve has been integrated into the Macyville restoration project.

Chapter 74

Annie's heart swelled and she was overwhelmed with gratitude. At the end, even with so much on his mind, Alex had remembered to make copies of all his files with the intention of bringing them to her the day he died.

Copying the information from the USB drives onto two of hers, she gave the originals back to Cheryl. She listened to Alex's last audio description and asked Jason to install it just before visitors entered the room with the dove sculpture. Then she suddenly remembered what had been nebulously floating through her brain for so many months. Several hours later she called Ed.

"Hi, Annie, I'm in a meeting with Carrie. We're almost finished; can I call you back?"

"This won't wait Ed. It's urgent."

Ten minutes later, she was sitting in Carrie's office. She explained that Cheryl Butler had found Alex's missing USB drives, there were two of them, not one, in his rain jacket pocket in her coat closet.

"A little while ago, Cheryl brought the drives to the museum. One contains all his Macyville files including the list he promised of the Butler, Cooper, and Ward descendants and the other, the audio conclusion he'd narrated for the exhibit. After Jason installed it, I downloaded a copy to my phone. I'd like you to listen to it."

Minutes later, she continued, "For months, I've had this uneasy feeling that had something to do with Macyville, but I couldn't put my finger on it. Things kept on happening, and I dismissed each incident never thinking it was part of a pattern.

"When we started our research for writing the grant, I discovered digitized newspaper articles at the library about the settlement. We used them for background to write the grant application, but at the time we didn't pay much attention to the specific details.

"As I was listening to the audio you just heard, I remembered reading an article about a local man who bought the property from the Macy family when they decided to retire to Florida in the 1970s. Then I did an online search and found it.

"The man who purchased the property was required to keep it as a nature preserve or for historic preservation, but he tried using his connections with our elected officials to get the land rezoned to build a resort community. He wasn't successful and ended up in jail for trying to bribe a trustee. Forced to sell the property at a significantly reduced price to the Conservancy, he went into bankruptcy.

"The bank took the family's large, historic home overlooking the lake and they moved to a small ranch in the country. The man's name was Clarence Swain; Robert and Steven are his grandsons.

"After re-reading that article, I did some more digging and discovered others dating back to the 1800s. It appears that ancestors of the same family attempted, without success, to purchase Macyville and were questioned numerous times about fires that started there shortly after they were rebuffed. No one could prove they were involved. I expect even if he knew about it, for obvious reasons, Alex couldn't mention their names in his audio description.

"Today it all came back to me. I remembered that shortly after we gained possession of the land from The Nature Conservancy, I received a call from a man named Steve who said he was inquiring about purchasing several acres of land near Freedom Hill for a cousin who lived in Buffalo.

"The weekend before Alex was killed, I was working in my office when, in addition to Josh Ward, two other men came in to take the tour. I heard them introduce themselves to Todd, our docent, but at the time the names didn't register, so I didn't think anything more about it.

"I called Todd before I came here and asked if he remembered that day, and he did. He recalled taking three men on a tour of the exhibit. One of them was Josh Ward and the others, who never gave him their last names, identified themselves as Bob and Steve.

"He was a bit non-plussed because they asked a lot of unusual questions about Macyville and wanted to view the architectural drawings and plot plans, which he couldn't show them—the contractors had them. Shortly after that, Robert called me to ask for a booth at the Festival of Lights, which as you all know I denied.

"Carrie, I know you'll remember that when Ed and I visited Charles Merrill in Toronto for Thanksgiving, he took us to a museum where I learned that Betsey Cooper had been enslaved at the Swain Plantation in Charleston. The name of the plantation triggered something in my brain; I suspected, incorrectly, that the Swain brothers might have been responsible for Alex's death. Still, something about their name continued to bother me.

"When we attended our friends' engagement party in Rochester the first weekend in January, I was waiting in line for a glass of wine and started chatting with a man who was interested in buying waterfront property in Lighthouse Cove to build a vacation home. He had driven by Macyville and asked about it. I suggested he contact a realtor who might help him after explaining that the property wasn't for sale. It had nothing to do with him, but I felt uneasy about the conversation and couldn't figure out why.

"Shortly after the party, Jason and I drove to the site to check the construction progress and intercepted two men who were taking photos with their cell phones. Something about them seemed familiar and I asked them if we'd met. They said we hadn't, but I wasn't so sure. Ed, I mentioned that to you and Brad when you joined me for lunch that day. Today I realized that they were correct; we hadn't met, but I'd recognized their voices from the other times I'd spoken to them.

"I'm certain there was a hidden motive for why the Swain brothers formed CFP. If they succeeded in getting their candidates elected to our various village boards, they expected zoning laws to be changed and they'd be able to purchase Macyville because they believed we wouldn't have money to rebuild it after it was destroyed by fire—a fire they intend to set."

Carrie listened, wide-eyed and incredulous. "Annie, this sounds like a plot for a British TV crime series. I know you're desperate for us to solve the case, but really?"

Ed defended his wife. "Carrie, you know as well as I do from working with Annie in the past, that she's not subject to flights of fancy. If she says the Swains are planning to destroy Macyville, I believe her. We need to call Chris Bayley and let Annie tell him what she suspects. This is way beyond the scope of what our police force can handle."

Carrie responded, "Josh Ward said he and Chris were working together on a case; perhaps this is the one."

"Josh Ward? What does he have to do with the FBI?" Annie asked. "I thought he was a realtor."

"Annie, when we interviewed Josh, we learned that that he's a retired FBI agent who sometimes works on special assignment with the Bureau. I'm sorry I couldn't tell you about it. Carrie, Brad, and I were sworn to secrecy," Ed replied.

Chapter 75

"I planned on calling you later this afternoon as a courtesy, Carrie," Chris Bayley said, minutes later as he, Josh and the others were seated around the table in her office.

"We arrested Robert and Steven Swain this morning after finding plot plans, incendiary devices, and other proof that they were planning to set fire to Macyville on July 3 during the village fireworks. They've been charged with conspiracy to commit domestic terrorism and will be arraigned by tomorrow morning."

He smiled at Annie, "If you ever decide to leave the museum, please give me a call. You'd make a terrific FBI agent. I'm in awe of your deductive reasoning skills."

Annie rolled her eyes, and adding a touch of levity to the situation, responded, "That's very flattering, Chris. When I leave the museum, my next job will be as a retired old lady sitting on some tropical beach in the winter, drinking Pina coladas with Ed."

They all laughed.

Annie asked, "How did *you* figure it out?"

"I met the Swains at the museum the Saturday before Alex was killed. We took the tour of the Macyville exhibit together," Josh responded.

"Like Todd, I thought their questions were a bit odd, and my radar went up. The tour ended; we walked out of the building together, making small talk. When they learned I was a realtor, they invited me to become a member of their group.

"I feigned interest, pretended to support their mission but expressed skepticism that CFP would have enough clout, even if their candidates were elected, to affect any measurable changes in zoning laws. They confided they had back-up plans to assure success, and while they weren't specific, I could read between the lines. I called Chris, he received permission from the home office to hire me to work undercover. We obtained a warrant to track their credit card expenses and records of their emails and phone calls, and you know the rest."

Carrie asked, "Can you share any of the details of how they planned it?"

"All of it," Chris answered, "but it stays inside this room."

Josh was scheduled to show a property to a client and excused himself. Chris filled in the blanks.

Chapter 76

When the historical society received the grant to rebuild Macyville, the Swain brothers, as Annie had surmised, were reminded about what had happened to their grandfather. For years they'd heard stories about how family fortunes were affected because Clarence hadn't been able to develop the land he purchased where the settlement had been.

To add to that, both brothers were strapped for cash. Robert had recently retired as a structural engineer for a firm in the city and was going through a bitter and costly divorce. Steven had worked as a web developer for a company that had downsized and relocated to North Carolina, and he was laid off. He'd had a difficult time finding another job.

"As you know, the men have a cousin, a real estate developer, who lives in Buffalo. He's built upscale condos and single-family homes in resort areas along Lake Erie and Georgian Bay and was looking for a site somewhere along Lake Ontario."

"He's the one who verified their alibi when Brad interviewed them," Ed interrupted, and Chris nodded.

"And the one Steven alluded to when he called me to inquire about subdividing the property," Annie said.

"Yes, that's correct. Robert and Stephen told him about Lighthouse Cove and invited him for a visit. He immediately coveted the Macyville property when they showed it to him. They knew that The Nature Conservancy had deeded the property to the Historical Society to rebuild the settlement, but the cousin said if they could find a way for him to purchase even a portion of it, he would give them generous finders' fees plus make them site managers of the project."

"Was the cousin involved in the plot?" Annie asked.

"He was not. FBI agents who work at the Buffalo office questioned him. When he learned the property was not available, he purchased acreage across the lake between Toronto and Kingston but mentioned to his cousins that he'd still be interested in acquiring the land if it ever became available. He jokingly remarked that he expected it would take an act of God, like fire from a lightning strike or flooding for that to happen. It gave the brothers an idea.

"As you are aware, the annual Lighthouse Cove Independence Day fireworks display occurs on the evening of July 3, instead of on the 4th, for several reasons. Thousands attend, the beaches and parks are packed, boaters congregate on the bay, and friends and family gather on their decks and porches to view the spectacle.

Chris continued, "Police, fire and ambulance personnel converge in the village from throughout the county in case of an emergency. The Swains decided that they would have their own fireworks that night, too, and they planned for the first buildings at Macyville to go up in flames about the same time as the fireworks started here.

"By the time anyone reported it, the settlement would be destroyed, and, as Annie correctly surmised, they expected the historical society wouldn't have funds to rebuild it. Misguided as it was, they truly believed their candidates running for office would be victorious during the primaries in April and again in November; after that they'd come swooping in to rescue you, Annie, by offering to buy the property, multi-purpose uses now permitted because of changes in zoning laws.

"They never imagined they'd get caught; they were certain their method of setting the fires would be hard to detect. Our fire inspectors are top-notch, and I'm positive if we hadn't uncovered their plan before they initiated it, we would have caught them. I'm glad it didn't get to that point."

Annie scoffed. "Well, they certainly aren't as smart as they think they are. Even if the zoning laws changed, we have a legal agreement with the National Trust and Conservancy that prohibits any sort of profitable development. We're also required to carry an insurance policy on all our properties: the museum, the Garden House that Amanda Reynolds deeded to us, and Macyville.

"Alex's maternal great-grandfather was a steel industry executive in Pittsburgh in the 1950s. Around that time the family established a charitable trust; it's administered by a well-respected law firm that's been in practice for generations. Before we even started writing the grant application, Alex contacted them to see whether, if we were successful in getting the grant, the trust would be willing to pay for the insurance. They were, for all properties in perpetuity. Even if Macyville had been destroyed, we'd have had the money to rebuild it."

Ed said, "I'm sorry I ever doubted you, Annie. You seemed to be obsessing about their name, and I was perplexed about it. I should have learned after these many years to trust you. Your instincts are almost always spot on."

"You're forgiven." She paused. "What's wrong with these people? All our hard work could have gone up in a fireball because of their greed, and as with Alex's murder, a desire for vengeance. What a bunch of cowardly, disgusting…"

Ed put his hand on hers. "It didn't happen," he said calmly and looked at Chris Blake. "Thank you. And please, when you speak with Josh again, thank him for us as well."

Chapter 77

"There's enough irony here to keep Popeye in spinach for eternity, Ed," Annie said two hours later as they were sitting at the kitchen table eating takeaway Cobb salads that they'd picked up at The Brewery.

Ed barked out a laugh. "That's quite a non-sequitur, Annie. What are you talking about?"

"Think about it, Ed. It all goes back to Josh Ward. Alex's murder and the plot to destroy Macyville would never have been solved without him. He was pivotal to both investigations.

"If he hadn't been in the museum the Saturday before Alex's death, I wouldn't have heard him introduce himself, and he wouldn't have met the Swains. If he hadn't listed the house Eve and Henri bought, I wouldn't have wondered where I'd heard his name before.

"Then we went to Glenellen and I saw his photo and read the headline about him and his brother having green eyes and I insisted that you interview him. If you hadn't, you wouldn't have learned about Kayla, which led you back to Jill as Alex's killer.

"And Cheryl wouldn't have learned that Alex was going to tell her about Kayla when they spoke before he was killed. The final irony is that Josh was working with Chris on the case neither of them could tell you about until it ended with the Swains being arrested."

"You figured that one out, Annie, so he can't take all the credit."

"I did, but he and Chris were one step ahead of me. I suppose if I hadn't called you and told you what I suspected and after that you called Chris, we might not have learned their motives, only that they'd been caught before they destroyed Macyville.

"In the end, I suppose it wouldn't have mattered, but knowing the details helps put all those unsettled feelings

I've had for months to rest. I was starting to feel a little paranoid and a bit crazy."

Chapter 78

Ed called Cheryl Butler a week later to check on her. She said she was doing better and had news to share.

The Wards had called her. They said they had finally told Kayla she was adopted, and although they dreaded letting her know that her birth mother was a murderer felt obligated to tell her about Alex. They had also contacted Joan Clark, who was delighted to learn that she had a granddaughter—Alex had always been one of her favorites. When given permission, she reached out to the young woman, and the two seem to have formed a close bond.

They said that Kayla was getting a lot of support from her husband, Andy, and had started seeing a therapist to help her work through her sadness and anger about what Jill had done and the fact that her parents had not told her about her adoption when she was younger. Once she understood the circumstances, she forgave them and accepted that they had wanted her so badly that they promised to not ever reveal who her birth parents were.

Cheryl offered to contact Kayla when they felt it was appropriate, but the couple suggested it might be better to wait and see what their daughter wanted to do. Shortly after the conversation, Kayla called to introduce herself. She wanted to learn more about her biological father.

Cheryl told Ed she'd invited her to visit and meet her half-siblings, who when they were told they had a half-sister, were delighted to welcome her into the family.

She learned about Alex through anecdotes, photos, and happy family stories, but refused to contact Jill, which was for the best. Jill never wanted her and would have caused more emotional distress to the young woman.

Later that day, Ed told Annie about Cheryl's call, and then called Carrie, who passed on the information to

Brad. They were pleased with the outcome and vowed to never let anyone know that Ellen Ward had at one time contemplated killing Alex. That was a secret they would take to their graves.

Chapter 79

Because of her nursing background, Jill was assigned to work in the prison infirmary. After she finished her duties, she spent most of her days alone. She refused to befriend the other inmates, believing they were beneath her. At first, members of her church and her minister reached out to her, but she made it clear that they were not welcome, and after a time those visits stopped.

Although she'd been a model prisoner, helpful, responsible, and pleasant, as Carrie had predicted, she was never granted parole. Fifteen years later, she appeared before a three-person parole board. Expressing remorse for what she'd done, all the while dabbing at her eyes, she almost convinced them she was rehabilitated, but they could sense an unbridled core of anger inside her, like a furious genie trying desperately to get out of its bottle.

While she was talking, the warden had entered the room and stood quietly by the door until she finished, then presented the panel with a stack of letters his staff had intercepted over the years. Jill had written threatening and angry diatribes to Cheryl Butler, the Wards and even her mother who, now deceased, had sold her home, and moved into a retirement community in Florida, never to return to Lighthouse Cove.

Furious when the panel declined her request for parole, Jill insisted that when she pled guilty, she'd been promised she'd receive it after fifteen years. The chair of the panel read the signed agreement that merely indicated that her case would be reviewed at that time, and if the board felt she could go back into society without endangering anyone, she'd be released. That clearly was not the case, she said, and they couldn't put the targets of her vitriol at risk. She had already killed once without remorse, and they had no doubt she'd do it again. While incarcerated, Jill had continued to smoke, at times quite heavily. She died of acute emphysema three years later at age 70.

Chapter 80

March was the month the locals called Mud Season, when torrents of melting snow flooded the curbs and gullies while racing toward the lake, leaving in their wake damp basements, swampy yards and, along the shoreline, a beach as mucky as quicksand.

A few days before March roared headlong into April, the DeCleryks hosted a dinner party to honor Alex Butler and celebrate solving the murder case and the plot to destroy Macyville. The day was chilly, the wind barreling in from the northeast, and the sky was thick with threatening dark clouds.

The rooms at the back of the house faced the lake, which, as dusk encroached upon daylight, was a study in contrasts. Out on the horizon the sky was clear, the sun shone low in the sky and cast a fierce orange glow above the deep, cobalt blue water. Halfway between the horizon and Lighthouse Cove, it peeked through fast moving clouds the color of burnished old pearls, the water a light, teal green. Closer to shore, moisture-laden storm clouds began releasing huge white flakes that melted into smoke-gray water that spewed dirty waves onto the beach.

A fire roared in the fireplace, the smell of butternut squash lasagna, redolent with sage and garlic, wafted through the kitchen as the they awaited their guests: Brad and his fiancée, Felicia; Cheryl Butler and her son, Daniel, who was home from college for the weekend; and Carrie and Matt Ramos, who were the first to arrive.

Ed and Annie ushered the police chief and her husband into the living room. "There's a tray with a roasted red pepper and walnut spread called Muhammara; olives; crudités, and toasted pita chips on the sideboard in the dining room.

"Go ahead and grab a plate. Ed will take your drink orders, then we can sit in the living room and talk before the others get here."

A few minutes later, the four friends were seated comfortably on chairs that had been placed near the fireplace, drinking glasses of Cabernet Sauvignon.

"You look fabulous, Carrie," Annie remarked, as she entered the room. "Much more rested. What's going on?"

"I'm not quitting my job. Matt came up with a perfect solution so I can keep it without being exhausted all the time.

"My parents will be retiring this summer and moving into the cottage next to us; it's been on the market for several months, and they just bought it. They'll help care for the kids when we need extra help. Matt's parents are retiring next year and have decided to move up here, too, so our children will get to know all their grandparents, and we'll have lots of family support while we raise them."

Annie hugged Carrie. "I'm so happy for you, Carrie. Both Ed and I were miserable thinking we'd lose you to the police academy."

A few minutes later, the rest of the group arrived. Ed took their drink orders, and Annie directed them to the platter of hors d'oeuvres—Gretchen beside her, wagging her tail in welcome. Each guest in turn bent down to pet her, and she licked their hands. Forty-five minutes later, they sat down to eat.

Cheryl announced that a celebration of life service for her husband would be held the Sunday of Memorial Day weekend in the gardens at Peace Church, when the snowbirds were back, and the weather was predictable. After that, the conversation centered around remembrances of Alex and the impact he'd made on Lighthouse Cove, as a loving husband and father, from his days as school superintendent, to his work as mayor and, finally, his initiative that resulted in the restoration of Macyville and Freedom Hill. His presence, a calming and comforting one, radiant with love, was felt throughout the room.

Epilogue

A few days later, Annie opened her computer and retrieved the file that contained the list Alex had created of relatives he'd discovered who were descended from his Macyville ancestors. She'd written a letter to inform them about his death and folded it into the invitation along with a reply card.

She'd been able to track down some of the remaining Macy family heirs who years ago had relocated to Florida and invited them to the grand opening. They were delighted when they learned the settlement had been restored and said they planned to attend. The patriarch, Edgar Benjamin Macy, a retired judge now in his 80s, sent a large donation and agreed to serve as the honorary chair.

But for a few who couldn't travel because of old age or other factors, all those who had been invited showed up, coming from New York and surrounding states, and as far west as California and into northern Canada.

Black, white, and mixed race, many were green-eyed like their ancestors. The night of July 3rd the extensive family convened for a picnic at the site, forming an immediate bond and vowing to remain in touch with an annual reunion each year at Macyville.

On July 4th, scores of visitors entered through the Alex Butler Visitors' Center where they received maps of the property and strolled through the hall of artifacts and the exhibit about Macyville that had been moved there for permanency from the museum.

A plaque on one wall listed the original settlers and their descendants. The gift shop was filled with books, including the commemorative one that Annie had commissioned, crafts, pottery, and replicas of antique jewelry. The snack bar offered authentic snacks and meals that Macyville residents would have eaten, sourced from local ingredients.

Dressed in period costumes, docents gave tours of the blacksmith shop, apothecary, school, the Quaker meeting hall, bakery, infirmary, and the modest homes where the abolitionists had lived peacefully with freed people of color and the formerly enslaved persons who had settled at the site after the Civil War had ended.

Cheryl Butler's children participated in the festivities. At dusk, portraying each of Alex's four ancestors, Jesse and his wife, Sara; Leah, and Daniel led visitors down the path to the beach at Freedom Hill where 100 yards out on the lake, a replica of Samuel Weatherfield's schooner was anchored, a small band playing songs of the Underground Railroad from its deck.

The brilliant orange ball of sun had flattened and sunk beneath the horizon with a flash of green and minutes later as darkness encroached and the moon slowly rose in the east, visitors were treated to magnificent fireworks with images symbolizing the abolition movement, Macyville, and Freedom Hill, the waypoint where fugitives escaped from slavery to freedom in Canada.

The End

RECIPES

Annie, Ed's wife, enjoys cooking and happily shares some of the recipes she prepared for friends and family in *Murder at Freedom Hill*:

Curried Spinach Dip (Serves 12-14)

2 tsp. curry powder, or to taste
1 tsp. ground cumin, or to taste
1 pkg. (9 ounces), uncooked baby spinach or 1 10 oz. package frozen, chopped spinach, thawed, drained, and squeezed dry
¾ C. reduced-fat sour cream
½ C. plain non-fat yogurt
2 garlic cloves, finely minced
Salt and pepper to taste (optional)

In a small nonstick skillet over medium-high heat, combine the spices and stir until fragrant. Transfer to small bowl. In a food processor or blender, combine remaining ingredients, process until smooth and blend in the curry and cumin. Season to taste. Transfer the dip to a container with a cover, refrigerate at least an hour and up to 24 hours. Bring dip to room temperature before serving with crudites and or crackers.

Muhammara (Serves 8)

One 15 oz. jar of roasted red bell peppers (remove two peppers from jar)
1½ oz. whole grain pita (one small pita)
1 ½ T. extra virgin olive oil
1 T. pomegranate molasses

2 tsp. ground black popper
1 tsp. ground cumin (or to taste)
¾ tsp. Kosher or sea salt
1 large garlic clove, chopped
2/3 C. chopped, toasted walnuts.

Place pita in a food processor until coarsely ground. Add remaining ingredients except walnuts, process until smooth. Add walnuts, pulse until almost smooth, leave some small chunks. Serve with cut vegetables and flatbread.

Slow-Cooker Beef Stew and Vegetables
(Serves 4 with leftovers)

1 T. extra virgin olive oil
1 ½ pounds boneless chuck roast or bottom round, cut into 1 ½-inch cubes
Salt, pepper to taste
1-pound large carrots, scrubbed and cut into 1-inch pieces
1-pound parsnips, scrubbed and cut into ½ inch pieces
1-pound small red potatoes, halved or quartered
1 medium onion, chopped
1 garlic clove, minced
2 cups beef broth
¼ cup. Balsamic vinegar
2 tsp. dried Italian seasoning, or a mixture of oregano and basil

Heat oil in large skillet over medium-high heat. Season beef lightly with salt and pepper. Add to skillet and cook, stirring occasionally, until browned on all sides. Place in 5–6-quart slow cooker with carrots, parsnips, and potatoes.

Add onion to same skillet with additional oil if necessary. Cook until onion is soft, 4-5 minutes. Add garlic and stir about 30 seconds. Add broth, vinegar and Italian seasoning and stir to scoop up any brown bits on the bottom of the skillet. Transfer to slow cooker and cook, covered, for 5 ½-6 hours on low or on high for 3 hours.

Butternut Squash Lasagna (Serves 6-8)

Preheat oven to 450 degrees and oil two large shallow baking pans
3 lbs. butternut squash, quartered, seeded, peeled, and cut into ½-inch cubes
3 T. vegetable oil
4 C. milk
2 T. dried rosemary, crumbled
1 T. minced garlic
½-stick unsalted butter
¼ C. all-purpose flour
Nine 7x3 1/2-inch sheets dried, no boil lasagna
1 1/3 C. freshly grated or shredded Parmesan
1 C. heavy cream
½ tsp. salt
Garnish with fresh rosemary sprigs if desired.

In a large bowl toss squash with oil until well coated and spread in one layer in pans. Roast for 10 minutes and season with salt. Stir and roast 10 minutes more or until tender and beginning to turn golden. While squash is roasting, bring milk and rosemary to a simmer in a saucepan. Cook over low heat for 10 minutes and pour through a sieve into a large heatproof pitcher or measuring cup. In a large heavy saucepan, cook garlic in butter over moderately low heat, stirring, until softened.

Stir in flour and cook, stirring, for three minutes. Remove pan from heat and add milk mixture in a stream, whisking occasionally, 10 minutes or until thickened. Stir in square and salt and pepper to taste. *Sauce may be made three days ahead and chilled, its surface covered with plastic.* Reduce temperature to 375 degrees and butter a 13x9x2 baking dish. Pour one cup sauce into dish (will not cover bottom completely) and cover with three lasagna sheets, making sure they do not touch. Spread half remaining sauce over pasta and sprinkle with ½ C. Parmesan. Make one more layer in the same manner and top with remaining three lasagna sheets.

In a bowl with electric mixer, beat cream with salt until it holds soft peaks and spread evenly over lasagna, completely covering pasta. Sprinkle remaining 1/3 C. Parmesan over cream. Cover dish tightly with foil, tenting slightly to prevent foil from touching cream, and bake in the middle of the oven for 30 minutes. Remove foil and bake 10 minutes more, or until bubbling and gold. Let stand 5 minutes before serving.

Whole Wheat Orange Quick Bread (Serves 10)

Preheat oven to 350 degrees
1 ½ C. whole wheat flour
¾ C. sugar
2 tsp. baking powder
¾ C. orange juice
½ C. canola or other vegetable oil
1 ½ C. all-purpose flour
2 T. grated orange peel
½ tsp. salt
½ C. milk (can use plant-based milk)
1 egg
½ C. chopped nuts, optional

Combine all ingredients in a mixing bowl. Stir until dry particles are moistened. Pour batter into greased, 9x5 or 8x4 loaf pan. Sprinkle with mixture of 1 T. sugar and ½ tsp. cinnamon, if desired. Bake for 60-65 minutes or until toothpick inserted into center comes out clean. Cool on rack before turning out of pan.

Provençale Sandwiches with Tuna, Basil, and Tomato (Serves 6)

½ C. red wine vinegar
6 flat anchovy fillets, rinsed, patted dry and minced
2 garlic cloves, minced
1 C. extra virgin olive oil
2 eight-inch rounds crusty bread
2 C. thinly sliced radishes
2 C. loosely packed fresh basil leaves
1 C. minced onion, soaked in cold water for 10 minutes, then drained
2 6 ½ oz. cans tuna in oil, drained and flaked
4 good ripe tomatoes, sliced thin

In a bowl, whisk the vinegar, anchovies, garlic and salt and pepper to taste. Add in oil in a stream, whisking until emulsified. Halve breads horizontally and hollow out halves until there's a ½ inch shell in each. Spoon one fourth of dressing evenly into each half. Working with one loaf at a time, arrange half the radish in one bottom shell and top with one fourth the basil. Arrange half the tomatoes on basil and fit top shell over tomatoes. Assemble another sandwich in same manner. Secure the sandwiches in plastic wrap and place on a shallow baking pan. Top sandwiches with a baking sheet and a large bowl filled with 2-pound weights (or something else that's heavy like soda cans) and chill for an hour. May be made 4 hours ahead. Cut sandwiches into wedges before serving.

Butter-Rich Fudge Brownies (Makes 12-16)

Preheat oven to 350 degrees
Butter and flour a 13x9x2 inch baking pan
4 oz. unsweetened chocolate
2 sticks unsalted butter, softened
2 C. sugar
3 large eggs
1 tsp. vanilla
1 C. sifted all-purpose flour
¾ C. chopped walnuts

In a small, heavy saucepan, melt chocolate and one stick butter over low heat, stirring, and cool completely. In a large bowl with an electric mixer, beat together remaining butter and sugar until light and fluffy. Add eggs, one at a time, beating well after each addition, and stir in chocolate mixture and vanilla. Add flour and a pinch of salt, stirring until well blended, and stir in walnuts. Pour batter into prepared pan, smoothing top, and bake in middle of oven 30-40 minutes until it pulls away slightly from sides of a pan and tester comes out with crumbs adhering to it. Cool brownies before cutting into squares. Can be made three days ahead, covered, and kept at room temperature.

ABOUT THE AUTHOR

 Karen Shughart studied English Literature at SUNY Buffalo, received a B.A. in Comprehensive Literature from the University of Pittsburgh, and completed graduate courses in English Literature from Shippensburg University.

She is the author of two non-fiction books and has worked as an editor, publicist, photographer, journalist, teacher, and non-profit executive. *Murder at Freedom Hill: An Edmund DeCleryk Mystery*, is the third in the series featuring the retired police chief and his intrepid wife, Annie. The first in the series is *Murder in the Museum*; the second, *Murder in the Cemetery*.

Before moving to a small village on the southern shore of Lake Ontario, Karen and her husband, Lyle, resided in south central Pennsylvania, near Harrisburg.

To sign up for Karen's blogs and newsletters or for more information, please visit her website at: www.karenshughart.com.

Made in the USA
Middletown, DE
11 November 2022

14677954R00146